Faust

Ivan Turgenev

Translated by Hugh Aplin

ET REMOTISSIMA PROPE

100 PAGES

100 PAGES

Published by Hesperus Press Limited
4 Rickett Street, London SW6 1RU
www.hesperuspress.com

Faust first published in Russian in 1856;
Yakov Pasynkov first published in Russian in 1855
This translation first published by Hesperus Press Limited, 2003

Introduction and English language translation © Hugh Aplin, 2003
Foreword © Simon Callow, 2003

Designed and typeset by Fraser Muggeridge
Printed in the United Arab Emirates by Oriental Press

ISBN: 1-84391-043-8

CONTENTS

In Chekhov's *The Seagull*, the famous writer muses moodily on his status as an artist, imagining his own tombstone: 'Here lies Trigorin. He was a good writer; but not as good as Turgenev.' By a curious twist of literary fortune, Turgenev's tombstone might just as well read: 'He was a good writer, but not as good as Chekhov.' There is a lazy perception that both as a short-story writer and – of course – as a dramatist, Turgenev is a somewhat less successful precursor of Chekhov, that the older writer's gentle, probing and subtle account of Russian life lacks the profound sense of absurdity and the penetrating dissection of the patterns of behaviour of a doomed society which render the younger man's work so vivid to us in the twenty-first century. The greatness of Turgenev's novel *Fathers and Sons*, with its uniquely eloquent record of the growing alienation of the younger generation from its parents, is readily acknowledged; but the special atmosphere of Turgenev's writing in general is less widely identified.

This is a great loss. It is a unique voice, and a unique oeuvre, and comparisons between the two writers reveal worlds of difference: on the one hand Turgenev, the comfortably-off scion of land-owning stock appalled by the savage brutality of his own class, intellectually sophisticated, amorously vulnerable, cosmopolitan, effortlessly fluent in French and German, internationally admired, at the forefront of his generation of writers, wrestling heroically with the political ideas of his time, a focus for the rage of both left and right, his funeral the last great gathering of all the classes in St Petersburg; on the other Chekhov – son of a bankrupt, a working doctor, committed in the most practical way to the reform of conditions among the disadvantaged, slowly emerging into literary fame, battling with remorseless ill-health, until he dies at the age of forty-four as the master-dramatist of his age, author, in the course of six years, of four incomparably fine and profoundly influential plays, all expressing, in one way or another, the death throes of an entire class. By the time Chekhov was writing his plays, the outcome of the struggle that led to the revolution of 1917 was almost a foregone conclusion: his characters are for the most part waiting to be swept away by the coming tidal wave, and his response was one of resigned irony very far from Turgenev's anguished attempt at sustaining a decently liberal position in the face of rising fanaticism.

There are points of comparison, however. A common thread is the theatre. Both men started their literary careers by writing theatrical pot-boilers – Chekhov churning out vaudeville sketches, Turgenev writing satires. Both then sought to refine their approaches to the stage. Turgenev wrote, in quick succession, *Alien Bread* and *A Month in the Country*, radically dispensing with melodramatic plots, focusing on character and atmosphere, conveying the texture of real life. Both these plays were suppressed by the censor, and *A Month in the Country* only achieved success twenty-seven years after he wrote it. It has since become a lynchpin of the repertory. *Alien Bread*, newly named *Fortune's Fool*, has had a recent triumphant run on Broadway, *Fathers and Sons* has been adapted for the stage with some success, and Turgenev himself puts in a wearily elegant appearance in Tom Stoppard's recent trilogy, *The Coast of Utopia*.

For all this, Turgenev is scarcely a major dramatist. But his skill with dialogue in his novels and his stories is an undoubted legacy of his work in the theatre, and clearly presages Chekhov's technique of interweaving random and unrelated threads of conversation. There is a characteristic passage in *Yakov Pasynkov*:

'Anton Nikitich,' came the voice of a maid from the hallway, 'would you bring a glass of water quickly for Sofia Nikolayevna.' 'What is it?' answered the pantryman. 'She seems to be crying…' I shuddered and went into the drawing-room for my hat. 'What were you and Sonechka talking about?' Varvara asked me indifferently; then, after a short silence, added in a low voice: 'There goes that clerk again.' I started taking my leave. 'But where are you going? Wait: Mummy will be out in a minute.' 'No, I can't, really,' I said, 'better another time.' At that moment, to my horror, and I mean horror, Sofia stepped firmly into the drawing-room. Her face was paler than normal, and her eyelids were just a little red. She did not even glance at me. 'Look, Sonya,' said Varvara, 'some clerk keeps walking about outside our house.' 'Some sort of spy…' remarked Sofia coldly and scornfully. This was simply too much! I left and really cannot remember how I dragged myself home.

The technique may be similar to Chekhov's, but the voice is quite distinct. It is always highly personal. To a remarkable degree, Turgenev's work has autobiographical origins. Both *Yakov Pasynkov* and *Faust* contain echoes of Turgenev's own experiences during the period of his official exile to his estate in Spasskoye, some two hundred miles from Moscow, to which he was banished in 1852, the year in which he completed *A Sportsman's Sketches*. Their unvarnished account of the conditions of life in rural Russia, particularly of the peasantry, enraged the censor; Turgenev was, briefly, imprisoned, then banished. It was during these eighteen months in the country that he began to grow and mature as an artist.

Faust is highly personal in more ways than one. The very opening of the story consists of a detailed description of Spasskoye, its grounds and house, and concerns a man who returns wearily from a long period of peregrination – as Turgenev had just done – and falls in love with a young woman. He told the great singer Pauline Viardot, the passionate friend who was at the centre of his emotional life for over forty years, that he was always 'the unlucky lover' in his own stories. Like Turgenev, the hero of *Faust* is in early middle-age and has abandoned all thoughts of passionate fulfilment. He is melancholy, somewhat introspective, attempting to find a modus vivendi in which he will not be disturbed by uncontrolled emotion. Shortly after writing his *Faust* Turgenev confided in a letter to another female friend with whom he was briefly infatuated, the passionate and restless Countess Tolstaya (sister of the great novelist), that it had been written at a turning-point in his life. 'My heart was afire with the last flames of memories, hopes and youth,' he says. 'I still dreamed of happiness and did not wish to give up all hope, but now I have waved all that goodbye.'

After reading the story, Tolstaya had told him that she discerned two men at conflict within him. Replying, he admits as much: his mind had conceived the ambition of building 'a quiet nest', but his heart, still vulnerable to the lure of love, protested, reproaching his mind: 'what had *it* done to create a good and sensible life?' Whereupon the mind was 'forced into silence and to hang its head'. This self-consciously Shakespearean dramatisation of the war within him (compare Sonnet 47: 'Betwixt mine eye and heart a league is took, / And each doth good turns now unto the other') is entirely characteristic of the protagonist of the short story. It also is strikingly reminiscent of Turgenev's celebrated analysis of Hamlet and Don Quixote ('the two eternal human types', as he calls them). 'Doubting everything, Hamlet, of course spares not himself; his mind is too much developed to be satisfied with what he finds within himself. He is conscious of his weakness; but even this self-consciousness is power: from it comes his irony, in contrast with the enthusiasm of Don Quixote. Hamlet delights in excessive self-depreciation. Constantly concerned with himself, always a creature of introspection, he knows minutely all his faults, scorns himself, and at the same time lives, so to speak, nourished by this scorn.'

Faust is in epistolary form, and the tone of the letters – urbane, fanciful, self-indulgent – admirably conveys this Hamletian solipsism; Turgenev's genius is to show its tragic consequences. Beyond the human tale is a terrible parable about the dangerous power of art and imagination, and the folly of releasing emotion in someone who is incapable of dealing with it. Goethe's play, from which the story takes its title, had enormous significance for Turgenev. He discovered it during his heady student days in Berlin (where he once shared lodgings with the future anarchist, Bakunin). It was the time of his immersion in German thought and culture, an immersion which deeply affected his work and thought, making him one of the principal *zapadniki*, those of the Westernising tendency, who sought to turn their backs on the primitive barbaric Russia celebrated by the so-called Slavophiles and embrace European values. He never ceased to be preoccupied by Goethe's great, sprawling, all-inclusive masterpiece, and indeed, his first serious published work was an essay-review inspired by Vronchenko's translation of it, in which he says, suggestively, that the play's greatest virtue is that Goethe never resolves the hero's dilemma. One may add that the play has no moral, and exists in a state of continuous flux, dealing with and peculiarly capable of arousing complex and almost nameless emotions.

In Turgenev's story, the narrator falls in love with a young woman who has never been exposed to fiction or to any art; she is a virgin of the imagination. He introduces her to a world which destroys her. The last letter in the story, describing these events, reveals a narrator devastated by what he has done, charred by the flames he has ignited, and resigned to a quiet and circumscribed life. It is part of Turgenev's subtlety and originality that the expected parallels with Goethe's play do not materialise, unless one perceives the narrator's actions as in some measure diabolic. (Interestingly, though, in another passage from 'Hamlet and Don Quixote', Turgenev remarks that 'Hamlet embodies the doctrine of negation, that same doctrine which another great poet has divested of everything human and presented in the form of Mephistopheles.') The story is a pitiless indictment of self-absorption, and a large part of its force is that it is a self-criticism on Turgenev's part.

The sort of man he would perhaps have liked to have been is the subject of *Yakov Pasynkov*, another story of unlucky love, three times over. The fascination of the piece, however, is its portrait of the title character, generally held to be based on the great (and tragically short-lived) critic Vissarion Belinsky, the standard-bearer for Turgenev and all the *zapadniki*, so memorably described by Isaiah Berlin: 'A man of passionate and undivided personality, Belinsky went through violent changes of position, but never without having lived painfully through each of his own convictions and having acted upon them with the whole force of his ardent and uncalculating nature until they failed him, one by one, and forced him, again and again, to make a new beginning, a task ended only by his early death.' As rendered by Turgenev, the intensity of the narrator's love for Pasynkov is profoundly touching.

Once again, it is 'Hamlet and Don Quixote', such a key document in the understanding of Turgenev's mind and heart, that speaks most eloquently of the inspiring quality of such an individual; of course Belinsky/Pasynkov is the polar opposite of Hamlet, and by implication, of Turgenev: 'Don Quixote is entirely consumed with devotion to his ideal, for the sake of which he is ready to suffer every possible privation and to sacrifice his life; his life itself he values only insofar as it can become a means for the incarnation of the ideal, for the establishment of truth and justice on earth... To live for oneself, to care for oneself, Don Quixote would consider shameful. He lives – if I may so express myself – outside of himself, entirely for others, for his brethren, in order to abolish evil, to counteract the forces hostile to mankind – wizards, giants, in a word, the oppressors... Don Quixote is an enthusiast, a servant of an idea, and therefore is illuminated by its radiance.' Bazarov in *Fathers and Sons* is just such a visionary and idealist, of course, and much of the power of the novel comes from his disturbing presence among the people to whom Turgenev himself belonged.

In fact, Turgenev, the practised charmer, the *salonnier*, the slave of love, spoke both bravely and subtly for his fellow-human beings, a fact acknowledged by his fellow-Russians when his body was transported back to St Petersburg after his death in Paris in 1883. A vast crowd, in which mingled liberals and reactionaries, revolutionaries and anarchists, assembled, closely watched by a unit of five hundred Cossacks and sundry other members of the military. The following day, during the shambles of a memorial literary evening, amongst various clumsy speeches and some garbled poetry readings, the great actress Savina, who had been the first to see the potential of *A Month in the Country*, read from *Faust*, finally giving something of the flavour and the power of the man.

– Simon Callow, 2003

Note:
The extracts from Turgenev's essay 'Hamlet and Don Quixote' are taken from David Modell's translation of 1907, reproduced in *Shakespeare in Europe*, edited by Oswald LeWinter, Pelican 1965.

INTRODUCTION

More than any other of the great Russian writers of the nineteenth century, Ivan Turgenev was, by instinct and experience, a European. He spent the major part of his adult life abroad, and a list of his literary friends reads like the roll-call for a master-class in prose-writing of the age of Realism – Henry James, Gustave Flaubert, Emile Zola, Guy de Maupassant, to name but a few. As a member of the Russian nobility, he was reared on a rich European cultural diet; and he was, broadly speaking, sympathetic to the Westernisers in their great debate with the Slavophiles about Russia's position vis-à-vis Western Europe – a debate that was central to much of Russia's cultural history during his lifetime. It should therefore come as no surprise that Turgenev included many a reference to Western art, philosophy and literature in his writings. What may be surprising is that no major German names can be found to figure among the sample of friends listed above; yet this is actually just a matter of historical chance, for, as the title of this volume suggests, German literature was just as important for Turgenev as were, say, French and English. Indeed, if allusions, quotations and reminiscences are totted up, then it is Germany's greatest poet, Johann Wolfgang von Goethe, who proves to figure more frequently than any other foreign writer in Turgenev's wide range of reference. Not for nothing did the Russian label himself 'an inveterate Goethean'.

Turgenev's enthusiasm for things German can be traced back to his youth, when he spent the years from 1838 to 1841 studying at Berlin University. The city at that time was something of a philosophical and cultural Mecca for young Russians, and it was there that the still rather immature future writer made the acquaintance of such older luminaries as the Moscow University history professor Timofei Granovsky; Nikolai Stankevich, the immensely influential hub of a philosophical circle who died tragically of consumption in 1840 at the age of only twenty-seven; and the anarchist-to-be Mikhail Bakunin. While men such as these played important roles in Turgenev's general development, his specific fascination with German culture and, first and foremost, with Goethe would have been fired by meetings with the great man's one-time close friend, Bettina von Arnim, and his future

English biographer, G.H. Lewes. Certainly by the time he settled back in Russia, Turgenev was said to know the first part of his favourite work, Goethe's *Faust*, all but by heart, rather like the narrator of his own story of the same name.

His desire to propagate Goethe in Russia is attested to by his translations of various parts of the German's literary output, including the final scene from Part One of *Faust*, which he published in 1844. That same year a translation by Mikhail Vronchenko of the whole of Part One of *Faust* appeared in St Petersburg and prompted Turgenev to write a lengthy review, not only dealing with the merits of Vronchenko's labour, but also summarising his own opinions of Goethe and *Faust* as they stood at that time. These were not what they might have been just a year or two earlier, for under the influence of Vissarion Belinsky, the leading Russian critic of the day, Turgenev was now disapproving of the egotism, individualism, the *romanticism* he perceived as central to Goethe's tragedy. Nonetheless, he still regarded it as 'the fullest expression of the age when battle was finally joined between the old days and the new, and men acknowledged that nothing was unshakeable except for human reason and Nature'. In particular he valued highly the aspiration it embodied to be free of 'the yoke of tradition, scholasticism and any sort of authority in general'; Goethe, he wrote, 'was the first to stand up for the rights of the individual, passionate, limited man'.

Such, then, was the background against which Turgenev's story *Faust* was written just over a decade after the publication of this review. And although *Yakov Pasynkov*, the second story in this volume, may not have the same self-evident links with German culture as Turgenev's *Faust*, still much of its substance can be seen ultimately to stem from similar sources.

Turgenev wrote *Faust* between June and August 1856, for the most part while living at Spasskoye, his late mother's estate in Orel Province. The descriptions of the estate in the story closely resemble the reality of Spasskoye, the narrator's past is very similar to Turgenev's own, and there may have been a further autobiographical strand in the plot of *Faust*. For it was in 1854 that Turgenev first met his neighbour, Maria Tolstaya, the sister of Leo Tolstoy, at her nearby home, Pokrovskoye. She was already married, but such niceties never prevented Turgenev from forming attachments, as is amply demonstrated by his lifelong relationship with Pauline Viardot. The physical description of Vera, the heroine of *Faust*, is reminiscent of Maria, and the idea of Vera's ignorance of creative literature may have been suggested by Maria's indifference to poetry. It is certainly tempting to picture Turgenev charting his own feelings for his charming neighbour through the relations between his fictional characters, even though the denouements in life and fiction were to differ very markedly.

The key event in the plot of Turgenev's *Faust* is the reading of Goethe's *Faust* to the heroine by the narrator. Such literary communication was a regular motif in Turgenev's works in the 1850s; the reading of one of Alexander Pushkin's poems in *A Quiet Spot* (1854) leads to catastrophe; in *Rudin* (1856) the eponymous hero reads several works of German literature, including *Faust*, to the young Russian girl who loves him; and in *Asya* (1858) the narrator's declaiming of Goethe's *Hermann and Dorothea* has a remarkable impact on the enigmatic heroine. Less characteristic of Turgenev at this time, albeit not later on in his career, is the intrusion of a supernatural element in the development of the plot. This led to a degree of criticism from those of his contemporaries who insisted on the pre-eminence of realism in literature, but such disapproval might be countered with the argument that here the supernatural should actually be interpreted not literally, but psychologically, as the projection of the characters' troubled feelings about their situation.

In any event, the nature of the relationship between hero and heroine, the sense of guilt and resignation that pervades the story's conclusion, the self-centred, introspective character of the male protagonist – all these are elements immediately recognisable to those familiar with Turgenev's oeuvre as a whole. And these features are discernible to one degree or another in *Yakov Pasynkov* too.

Turgenev wrote this story in an even shorter time than *Faust*, in less than two weeks in February 1855, although he did make some significant changes between its first publication in a journal later that year and its subsequent reissue in book form. The most obvious of these was the exclusion of the story's epigraph, which had immediately forged a link with German culture, for it was a quotation from Friedrich von

Schiller – 'Dare to err and to dream'.

Work on *Yakov Pasynkov* was simultaneous with that on *Rudin*, and the interrelatedness of Turgenev's writings in the mid-1850s is suggested by the removal of the original opening of the former story to the latter and the transfer of the name Pasynkov in the opposite direction. Similarly, just as Turgenev drew on his own life as a student in Germany for the background of the narrator of *Faust*, so he used aspects of his own pre-Berlin life for the early biography of his narrator in *Yakov Pasynkov*. But a strong link with Germany is established in this story too through the figure of Yakov Pasynkov himself. Most obviously, he is a great admirer of German art, reading Schiller in the original and revering the music of Schubert. He is, indeed, in general a representative of the generation of young Russians who grew up under the influence of German idealism in the 1830s. Critics have identified the youthful Belinsky, before his move away from idealism, as the specific prototype for the character of Pasynkov; yet it might also be suggested that those Russians Turgenev knew in Berlin, such as Stankevich, already long dead, and Granovsky, who died in 1855, joined Belinsky (who had died in 1848) in Turgenev's consciousness to form a composite portrait of a doomed, but memorable romantic. Certainly the relationship between the story's narrator and its hero, Pasynkov, could be seen to echo that between Turgenev and any one of these mentors.

But irrespective of its model, it is Pasynkov's very nature, with its burning sincerity, its enthusiasm, kindness and generosity, and its thirst for truth and beauty that is of supreme importance. It was the contrast between such a figure and the self-obsessed self-analysts whose introspection leads to the spiritual paralysis, pessimistic scepticism and misanthropy that Turgenev was to explore in his lecture 'Hamlet and Don Quixote' (1860). The conclusion he reached was that the actual achievement of a man is arguably of less significance than the nature of his aspirations and the manner of his life. This was a lesson that Turgenev had been taught by Granovsky in Berlin in the 1830s, and it was a belief held by Goethe too.

Turgenev is perhaps best known for his depiction of 'superfluous men', Russian Hamlets incapable of fulfilling their potential, and although he proved his own worth as one of the finest of all Russian novelists, he was himself close to this type in temperament. Yet his writings also include numerous examples of the optimistic, active idealist, the quixotic character, whose origins are for him to be traced no less to Germany than to Spain. The two stories in this volume reflect admirably the debt that Turgenev owed to German culture, while at the same time underlining his right to a place of honour not only on a Russian Parnassus, but on a European one too.

– Hugh Aplin, 2003

Faust

Entbehren sollst du, sollst entbehren. [1]

Faust (Part I)

FIRST LETTER

From Pavel Alexandrovich B*** to Semyon
Nikolayevich V***

THE VILLAGE OF M***OYE, 6TH JUNE 1850

I arrived here three days ago, my dear friend, and, as promised, I am taking up my pen and writing to you. There has been a sprinkling of light rain since the morning: it's not possible to go out and, what's more, I feel like having a little chat with you. Here I am again in my old nest, where I haven't been – it's frightening to say – for nine whole years. If you think about it, it really is as if I've become a different person. And actually I am different: do you remember, in the drawing-room, my great-grandmother's dingy little mirror with those strange little scrolls in the corners? You were always wondering what it had seen a hundred years ago. As soon as I arrived I went up to it – and became embarrassed in spite of myself. I suddenly saw how I've aged and changed of late. But then I'm not the only one that's aged. My little house, already long ramshackle, is now scarcely standing, it's grown crooked and sunk into the ground. My kind Vasilyevna, the house-keeper (you've not forgotten her, I'm sure: she fed you such marvellous jam), has become quite dried up and bent; when she saw me, she was unable to cry out and didn't burst into tears, but just started groaning, had a coughing fit, sat down on a chair in exhaustion and waved her hand. The old man, Terenty, is still in good form, stands up as straight as ever and twists his legs about when he walks, wearing the same funny yellow nankeen trousers and the same squeaky goatskin shoes with the high instep and bows that moved you on more than one occasion... But my God! How those trousers flap about now on his skinny legs! How white his hair has become! And his face has quite shrivelled up to the size of a small fist; and when he started to talk to me, when he began to make arrangements and give out orders in the room next door, I found it funny, and yet felt sorry for him too. He's lost all his teeth, and he speaks in a mumble accompanied by a whistling and a hissing. On the other hand the garden has become amazingly pretty: the modest little lilac, acacia and honeysuckle bushes (you remember, you and

3

I planted them) have filled out into magnificent dense shrubs; the birches and maples – they've all shot up and spread wide; the lime-tree walks have become particularly attractive. I love those walks, I love the delicate grey-green colour and the subtle scent of the air beneath their vaults; I love the dappled network of bright little circles across the dark earth – I have no sand, you know. My favourite oak sapling has already become a young oak tree. In the middle of the day yesterday I sat for more than an hour in its shade on a bench. I felt very happy. All around, the grass was so cheerful and flourishing; a golden light, strong and soft, lay on everything; it even penetrated into the shade… and the birds that could be heard! I hope you haven't forgotten that birds are my passion. Turtle-doves cooed incessantly, an oriole would whistle every now and then, a chaffinch played its sweet little trick, the thrushes got angry and twittered away, a cuckoo responded in the distance; suddenly, like a maniac, a woodpecker would utter its piercing cry. I listened, listened to all this soft, collective babbling, and did not want to stir, and it was hard to tell if it was idleness or emotion in my heart. And it's not just the garden that has grown: my eye is constantly being caught by solid, hefty lads, in whom I just cannot recognise the little boys I knew before. And your favourite, little Timosha, has now become such a grown-up Timofei, you just can't imagine. You were afraid for his health then and foretold consumption for him; but if you looked now at his huge red hands, the way they poke out of the tight sleeves of his nankeen frock-coat, and what rounded, thick muscles he has bulging everywhere! The back of his neck is like a bull's, and his head is covered in tight blond curls – a perfect Farnese Hercules! But then his face has changed less than those of the others, it hasn't even grown much in size, and his cheerful – 'yawning', as you used to say – smile has remained the same. I've taken him on as my valet; I got rid of the one from St Petersburg while in Moscow: he was so very fond of putting me to shame and letting his superiority as regards the ways of the capital be felt. I didn't find a single one of my dogs; they've all died off. Only Nefka lived longer than all the rest, but even she didn't stay around long enough, the way Argos waited for Ulysses; she was not fated to see her former master and hunting companion with her dim eyes. But Shavka is alive, and barks in the same hoarse way, and has one

4

ear torn in just the same way, and has burrs in her tail as she should. I've moved into your former little room. The sun beats into it, it's true, and there are a lot of flies in it; on the other hand there is less of the smell of an old house than in all the other rooms. It's a strange thing! That musty, slightly sour and faded smell has a powerful effect on my imagination: I can't say that I find it unpleasant, on the contrary; but it makes me sad and, in the end, depressed. Just like you, I am very fond of old, bow-fronted chests with brass finger-plates, white armchairs with oval backs and crooked legs, fly-blown glass chandeliers with a large egg-shaped piece of lilac foil in the middle – in short, all sorts of furniture from our grandfathers' time; but I can't see it day in, day out: a sort of uneasy boredom (that's it precisely!) takes hold of me. The furniture in the room I've moved into is the most ordinary home-made stuff; however, I've left a long, narrow chest of drawers in the corner, on which various pieces of antiquated green and blue blown glassware can scarcely be seen through the dust; and I've ordered to be hung on the wall, do you remember, that portrait of a woman that you called the portrait of Manon Lescaut[2]. It's become a little darker over these nine years, but the eyes look out just as pensively, slyly and tenderly, the lips laugh just as frivolously and sadly, and the rose with half its petals pulled off droops just as gently from her slender fingers. The curtains in my room are most amusing. They were once green, but have turned yellow in the sun: painted across them in black dye are scenes from d'Arlincourt's *The Hermit*[3]. On one curtain this hermit, with the most enormous beard and bulging eyes and wearing sandals, is enticing some dishevelled young lady away into the mountains; on the other a bitter struggle is taking place between four knights wearing berets and with padded shoulders; one is lying dead *en raccourci*; in short, every horror is represented, while all around there is such untroubled calm, and the curtains themselves reflect the light so meekly across the ceiling… A sort of spiritual hush has come upon me since I moved in here; I don't want to do anything, I don't want to see anyone, there's nothing to dream about, I'm too idle to have ideas – but I'm not too idle to think: these are two different things, as you know very well yourself. Memories of childhood crowded in on me at first… wherever I went, whatever I looked at, they rose up from all sides, clear, clear to the tiniest details, and seemingly fixed in their sharp definition... Then these memories were replaced by others, then... then I gradually turned away from the past, and there only remained a sort of drowsy weight in my breast. Imagine! Sitting on a weir underneath a willow tree, all of a sudden I unexpectedly burst out crying, and would have cried for a long time, despite my already declining years, if I had not been put to shame by a passing peasant woman, who gave me a curious look and then, without turning her face towards me, bowed straight and low and went on by. I should very much like to remain in a mood like this (it goes without saying that I won't be crying any more) right up until the time I leave here, until September, that is, and I should be most upset if any of the neighbours took it into their heads to call on me. But there seems to be no reason to fear that; I don't even have any near neighbours. I'm sure you'll understand me; you know from your own experience how beneficial solitude can often be... I need it now, after my various wanderings.

But I shan't get bored. I brought several books with me, and I have a respectable library here. Yesterday I opened up all the cabinets and spent a long time rummaging among the mouldering books. I found many curious things that I had not noticed before: *Candide* in a manuscript translation from the 1770s; newspapers and journals from the same time; *The Triumphant Chameleon* (Mirabeau, that is); *Le Paysan perverti* etc.[4] I came across children's books, both my own, and those of my father and grandmother, and even, imagine, my great-grandmother: one dreadfully tatty French grammar in a mottled binding has written on it in large letters: *Ce livre appartient à m–lle Eudoxie de Lavrine*[5], and the year is marked down as 1741. I saw the books that I once brought from abroad, among them Goethe's *Faust*. Perhaps you're not aware that there was a time when I knew *Faust* off by heart (the first part, it goes without saying), word for word; I couldn't read it enough... But new days, new ways, and in the course of the last nine years I've scarcely had occasion to pick Goethe up. With what an inexpressible feeling did my eyes light on the little book I know all too well (a poor edition from 1828)! I carried it off with me, lay down on the bed, and began to read. What an effect the entire magnificent first scene had on me! The appearance of the Earth Spirit, his words, you remember: 'On the waves of life, in the whirlwind of creation', aroused in me a tremor long unknown and a chill of rapture. I remembered everything: Berlin, my time as a student, Fräulein Klara Stich, and Seidelmann in the role of Mephistopheles, and Radziwill's music, and absolutely everything...[6] I couldn't get to sleep for a long time: my youth came and stood before me like a ghost; like fire, like poison it ran through my veins, my heart swelled and didn't want to contract, something tugged at its strings, and desires boiled up...

Those are the dreams that your friend of almost forty fell into, sitting all alone in his lonely little house! What if someone had been spying on me? Well, so what? I wouldn't have been ashamed at all. Being ashamed is a sign of youth as well; and do you know why I've begun to notice that I'm getting old? Here's why. I try now to exaggerate to myself my cheerful feelings and curb my sad ones, whereas in the days of my youth I did quite the reverse. You'd fuss over your sadness like a treasure, and be shamefaced about a burst of gaiety...

Yet it seems to me nevertheless, that regardless of all my experience of life, there is still something on this earth, my friend Horatio, that I haven't tried, and that that 'something' is all but the most important thing.

Huh, what have I ended up writing! Goodbye! Until the next time. What are you doing in St Petersburg? Incidentally, Savyely, my cook here in the country, asks to be remembered to you. He's aged as well, but not too much, he's grown rather fat and flabby. He's just as good at making chicken soup with boiled onions, curd tarts with decorative edging, and sour cucumber skilly, that renowned dish of the steppes that made your tongue turn white and go stiff for a whole day. On the other hand, his roast meat turns out just as dry as ever, so dry you can knock it about on your plate, but it's still like cardboard. Anyway, goodbye!

Your P.B.

SECOND LETTER

From the same to the same

I have quite an important piece of news to tell you, dear friend. Listen! Yesterday, before lunch, I felt like taking a walk, only not in the garden; I set off along the road to town. Taking great strides down a long straight road without any objective is very pleasant. It's as if you're doing something, hurrying somewhere. I look, and there's a carriage coming towards me. 'It's not going to my place, is it?' I thought in secret terror... But no: in the carriage sits a gentleman I don't know with a moustache. I was reassured. But suddenly this gentleman, drawing level with me, orders the coachman to stop the horses, raises his cap courteously, and even more courteously asks me am I not so-and-so, calling me by my name. I stop in my turn and with the enthusiasm of a man on trial who is being taken for interrogation I reply that 'I am so-and-so', while gazing like a sheep at the gentleman with the moustache and thinking to myself: 'But I've seen him somewhere, you know!'

'Don't you recognise me?' he says, climbing down from the carriage in the meantime.

'Not at all.'

'But I recognised you straight away.'

It turns out little by little that it was Priyimkov, you remember, our one-time companion at university. At this moment, dear Semyon Nikolayich, you're thinking: 'What sort of important piece of news is that then? Priyimkov, so far as I can recall, was a rather shallow fellow, albeit not vicious and not stupid.' That's all true, my good friend, but listen to how the conversation continued.

'I was very glad,' he says, 'when I heard you were visiting your village, right next door to us. But I wasn't the only one who was glad.'

'May I learn,' I asked, 'who else could have been so kind?...'

'My wife.'

'Your wife?'

'Yes, my wife: she's an old acquaintance of yours.'

'Well, may I learn your wife's name?'

8

'Her name is Vera Nikolayevna; her maiden name was Yeltsova…'

'Vera Nikolayevna!' I exclaim involuntarily…

And this is that very same important piece of news I told you about at the beginning of the letter.

But perhaps you find nothing important even in this… I shall have to tell you something from my past… from my life long past.

When you and I left university together in 183*, I was twenty-three years old. You entered the civil service; I, as you are aware, resolved to set off for Berlin. But there was nothing to do in Berlin any earlier than October. I took a fancy to spending the summer in Russia, in the countryside, to being good and idle for the last time, before then taking up work in earnest. To what extent this last assumption was realised – there's no point in enlarging on that now… 'But where am I to spend the summer?' I wondered. I didn't feel like going to my own village: my father had recently died, I had no close relations, I was afraid of loneliness, boredom… And so I gladly accepted the proposal of one of my relatives, a cousin once removed, to be his guest on his estate in the province of T***. He was a well-to-do man, kind and straightforward, he lived like a lord, and had a home like a palace. I moved in with him. My cousin's family was a large one: two sons and five daughters. And in addition there were masses of people living in his house. Guests were constantly dropping in – but it still wasn't much fun. The days flowed by noisily, there was no opportunity for privacy. Everything was done together, everyone tried to amuse themselves with something or other, to think something or other up, and by the end of the day everyone was dreadfully tired. There was something vulgar about that life. I was already beginning to dream of leaving and was only waiting for my cousin's name-day to pass, but on the name-day itself, at the ball, I saw Vera Nikolayevna Yeltsova – and I stayed.

She was then sixteen years old. She lived with her mother on a small estate about five kilometres from my cousin. Her father – a remarkable man, they say – had rapidly attained the rank of colonel and would have gone still further, but was killed as a young man, accidentally shot by a comrade while hunting. He left Vera Nikolayevna still a child. Her mother was an extraordinary woman too: she spoke several languages, knew a great deal. She was seven or eight years older than her husband, whom she married for love; he carried her away in secret from her parents' home. She scarcely survived losing him, and right up until her death (according to Priyimkov, she died soon after her daughter's wedding) wore only black dresses. I remember her face vividly: expressive, dark, with thick hair that had grown grey, large, severe eyes, in which the light seemed to have gone out, and a narrow, straight nose. Her father – his name was Ladanov – had lived for fifteen years or so in Italy. Vera Nikolayevna's mother was born of a simple peasant woman from Albano[7], who was killed the day after she gave birth by her fiancé, a Trasteverino[8], from whom Ladanov had stolen her… This story caused a great stir in its time. Returning to Russia, Ladanov never left his study, let alone his house, and occupied himself with chemistry, anatomy, secret spells, wanting to prolong human life, imagining it was possible to commune with spirits, summon up the dead… His neighbours considered him a wizard. He was extremely fond of his daughter, taught her everything himself, but did not forgive her for running away with Yeltsov, did not let either her or her husband into his sight, foretold a life of sorrow for both of them and died alone. Having been left a widow, Mrs Yeltsova dedicated all her free time to the upbringing of her daughter, and received almost nobody. When I made Vera Nikolayevna's acquaintance, just imagine, she had not been to a single town since the day she was born, not even the one in her own district.

Vera Nikolayevna did not resemble ordinary young Russian ladies: a certain particular imprint lay upon her. From the first I was struck by the astonishing calm in all her movements and speech. She did not seem to make a fuss about anything, did not become anxious, replied simply and intelligently, listened attentively. The expression on her face was sincere and truthful like that of a child, but somewhat cold and unchanging, although not pensive. She was gay but rarely, and not in the same way as others: the clarity of an innocent soul, more comforting than gaiety, shone throughout her being. She was of no great height, had a very good figure, was rather slim, had regular and gentle features, a fine, even forehead, golden-russet hair, a straight nose like her mother's, quite full lips; her darkly tinged grey eyes gazed too directly somehow from beneath fluffy, upward curving lashes. Her hands were not large, but not very pretty: people of talent don't have such hands… and indeed, Vera Nikolayevna did not have any particular talents. Her voice rang like that of a seven-year-old girl's. At my cousin's ball I was presented to her mother, and a few days later I went to visit them for the first time.

Mrs Yeltsova was a very strange woman with a strong character, insistent and intense. She had a powerful influence on me: I was both respectful and a little afraid of her. She had everything done according to a system, and she brought her daughter up according to a system too, but did not restrict her freedom. Her daughter loved her and had blind faith in her. Mrs Yeltsova only had to give her a book and say: 'don't read this page', and she would rather miss out the preceding page than risk glancing at the forbidden one. Yet Mrs Yeltsova had her *idées fixes* as well, her hobby-horses. For example, she feared like the devil anything that might affect the imagination; and so her daughter, right up to the age of seventeen, had not read a single story, nor a single poem, whereas in geography, history and even in natural history she would quite often have me stumped – me, a graduate, and quite a good one, as you perhaps recall. I once tried to have a talk with Mrs Yeltsova about her hobby-horse, although it was difficult to draw her into conversation: she was very taciturn. She only shook her head.

'You say,' she said finally, 'reading works of poetry is *both* useful *and* pleasant… I think one has to choose in life in advance: *either* the useful *or* the pleasant, and thus come to a decision once and for all. I too once wanted to combine both the one and the other… It is not possible and it leads to ruin or to vulgarity.'

Yes, that woman was an astonishing creature, an honest creature, proud, not without fanaticism and superstition of a sort. 'I'm afraid of life,' she said to me once. And she really was afraid of it, she was afraid of those secret forces on which life is built and which only occasionally, but suddenly, burst through to the surface. Woe betide the person over whom they rage! These forces had spoken to Yeltsova in a terrible way: remember the deaths of her mother, her husband, her father… That would have frightened anybody. Never did I see her smile. It was as if she had locked herself up and thrown the key into the water. She must have suffered much grief in her time and had never shared it with anyone: she hid it all away inside her. She had trained herself not to give

11

free rein to her feelings to such a degree that she was even ashamed of displaying her passionate love for her daughter; not once did she kiss her in my presence, never did she call her by a pet name, it was always: 'Vera'. I remember one remark of hers: I said to her once that we, people today, are all a little damaged... 'There's no point in damaging yourself a little,' she pronounced, 'you should break yourself completely or else not touch...'

Very few people called on Yeltsova, but I visited her often. I was secretly conscious that she was well disposed towards me, and I liked Vera Nikolayevna very much. She and I talked, went for walks... Her mother did not bother us; the daughter did not herself like to be without her mother, and I, for my part, did not feel any need for any private conversation either. Vera Nikolayevna had the strange habit of thinking out loud; in the night-time she would talk in her sleep loudly and distinctly about what had struck her in the course of the day. Once, after looking at me closely, leaning her cheek gently on her hand, as was her habit, she said, 'I think B. is a good man, but he can't be relied on.' Relations between us were the most amicable and equable; only once did it seem to me that I had discerned somewhere there, far away, in the very depths of her bright eyes, something strange, a certain languor and tenderness... But perhaps I was mistaken.

Meanwhile the days were passing, and it was already time for me to prepare for my departure. But I continued to linger. Sometimes, when I thought, when I remembered, that soon I would not be seeing this sweet girl to whom I had become so attached, I would start to feel awful... Berlin was beginning to lose its magnetic power. I did not dare to admit to myself what was happening inside me, and I did not even understand what was happening inside me – it was as if there were a mist adrift in my soul. Finally, one morning, everything suddenly became clear to me. 'What more am I to seek?' I thought. 'Where am I to aspire? After all, the truth is hard to come by. Wouldn't I do better to stay here and get married?' And just imagine, this idea of marriage didn't scare me at all at the time. On the contrary, I was glad of it. Moreover, that same day I announced my intention, only not to Vera Nikolayevna, as might have been expected, but to Yeltsova herself. The old woman looked at me.

'No, my dear,' she said, 'you go to Berlin, do a little more damage to yourself. You're kind; but a different sort of husband is needed for Vera.'

I dropped my eyes, blushed, and, what will probably surprise you still more, inwardly concurred with Yeltsova straight away. I left a week later, and since then I had never again seen either her, or Vera Nikolayevna.

I've described my experiences to you in brief because I know you don't like anything 'expansive'. After arriving in Berlin I very soon forgot Vera Nikolayevna… But, I confess, the unexpected news about her excited me. I was struck by the idea that she was so close, that she was my neighbour, that I would see her in a few days' time. The past had suddenly risen up before me, as though from out of the ground, it had drawn really close to me. Priyimkov announced to me that he had paid me a visit with the specific aim of renewing our old acquaintance and that he hoped to see me at his house in a very short time. He informed me that he had served in the cavalry, retired as a lieutenant, bought an estate eight kilometres from me and intended to farm, that he used to have three children, but two had died, and only a five-year-old daughter remained.

'And does your wife remember me?' I asked.

'Yes, she remembers you,' he replied, with a slight hesitation. 'Of course, she was still a child, you might say, then; but her mother was always full of praise for you, and you know what store she sets by the deceased's every word.'

Yeltsova's words that I was not suitable for her Vera came to mind… 'So *you* must have been suitable,' I thought, sneaking sidelong glances at Priyimkov. He spent several hours with me. He's a very good, nice fellow, he talks so modestly, looks so genially, it's impossible not to take a liking to him… but his mental capabilities have not developed since the time we knew him. I shall go and call on him without fail, perhaps even tomorrow. I'm extremely curious to see how Vera Nikolayevna has turned out.

You're probably laughing at me now, you villain, sitting at your director's desk: but I'll nonetheless write and tell you what impression she makes on me. Goodbye! Until the next letter.

Your P.B.

THIRD LETTER

Well, old fellow, I've visited her, I've seen her. First of all I ought to inform you of an amazing circumstance: believe it or not, as you wish, but she has hardly changed at all either in face or in figure. When she came out to meet me, I was lost for words: a girl of seventeen, no less! Only the eyes are not like a girl's; but then even when she was young her eyes were not those of a child, they were too light. But the same calm, the same clarity, the voice the same, not a single wrinkle on her forehead, as if she had been lying in the snow somewhere all these years. But she's twenty-eight years old now, and she's had three children... I don't understand it! Please don't think I'm exaggerating because I'm biased; on the contrary, I didn't like this 'immutability' of hers at all.

A woman of twenty-eight, a wife and mother, ought not to resemble a little girl: she's not lived for nothing. She greeted me very cordially, but my arrival simply delighted Priyimkov: that kind fellow just looks for a way to become attached to someone. Their house is very cosy and clean. Vera Nikolayevna was dressed like a little girl as well: all in white with a blue sash, and a delicate gold chain around her neck. Her daughter is very sweet and not at all like her: she brings her grand-mother to mind. In the drawing-room above the sofa hangs a portrait of that strange woman, amazingly like her. I was struck by it as soon as I went in. She seemed to be looking at me sternly and carefully. We sat ourselves down, reminisced about the old days, and little by little our conversation developed. I kept on involuntarily glancing at the gloomy portrait of Yeltsova. Vera Nikolayevna sat directly beneath it: that's her favourite place. Imagine my surprise: Vera Nikolayevna has still not yet read a single novel, or a single poem, in short, not a single – as she expresses it – invented work! This incomprehensible indifference to the most elevated pleasures of the mind made me angry. In a woman who is intelligent and, so far as I can judge, highly sensitive, it is simply unforgivable.

'What sort of rule is this,' I asked, 'that you've imposed on yourself, never to read such books?"

'I've not had occasion,' she replied, 'there's been no time.'

'No time! I'm amazed! You at least,' I continued, turning to Priyimkov, 'might have given your wife a taste for it.'

'With pleasure I –' Priyimkov began, but Vera Nikolayevna interrupted him.

'Don't put on a pretence: you're no great lover of poetry yourself.'

'Not really of poetry, indeed,' he began, 'but novels, for example…'

'But what do you do, how do you keep yourselves occupied in the evenings?' I asked. 'Do you play cards?'

'Sometimes we do,' she replied, 'but is there a shortage of things to occupy you? We read as well: there are good works other than poetry.'

'Why do you attack poetry so?'

'I'm not attacking it: I've been accustomed since childhood not to read these invented works; that was the way Mother wanted it, and the longer I live, the more convinced I become that everything that Mother did, everything she said, was the truth, the holy truth.'

'Well, as you wish, but I cannot agree with you: I'm convinced that you're depriving yourself to no purpose of the purest, the most legitimate pleasure. After all, you don't reject music, painting: why then do you reject poetry?'

'I don't reject it: I've not yet made its acquaintance – that's all.'

'Then I'll take that upon myself! It wasn't for the rest of your life that your mother forbade your acquaintance with works of belles-lettres, was it?'

'No; as soon as I married, my mother withdrew any sort of prohibition from me; it didn't occur to me myself to read… how did you put it?… well, in short, to read novels.'

I listened to Vera Nikolayevna in bewilderment: I had not expected this.

She looked at me with her calm gaze. Birds look like that when they're not afraid.

'I'll bring you a book!' I exclaimed. (The *Faust* that I had recently read came suddenly into my head.)

Vera Nikolayevna sighed quietly.

'It… it won't be George Sand[9]?' she asked, not without timidity.

15

'Ah, so you've heard of her? Well, perhaps even her, what does it matter?... No, I'll bring you another author. You haven't forgotten German, have you?'

'No, I haven't.'

'She speaks it like a German,' Priyimkov joined in.

'That's fine then! I'll bring you... well, you'll see what an amazing thing I'll bring you.'

'Alright then, I'll see. But now let's go into the garden, Natasha can't keep still otherwise.'

She put on a round straw hat, a child's hat, exactly the same as the one her daughter put on, only a little bigger, and we set off into the garden. I walked alongside her. In the fresh air, in the shade of the tall limes, her face seemed to me to be even prettier, especially when she turned slightly and threw her head back to look at me from under the brim of the hat. Had it not been for Priyimkov walking behind us, had it not been for the little girl skipping ahead of us, I truly could have thought that I was not thirty-five, but twenty-three; that I was still only preparing to go to Berlin, particularly as the garden we were in was very like the garden on Yeltsova's estate too. I could not restrain myself and conveyed my impression to Vera Nikolayevna.

'Everyone tells me that I've changed very little outwardly,' she replied, 'but then I've remained the same inwardly too.'

We went up to a small Chinese-style summer-house.

'We didn't have a house like this in Osinovka,' she said, 'but pay no attention to its being so crumbling and faded, it's very nice and cool inside.'

We went into the house. I looked around.

'Do you know what, Vera Nikolayevna?' I said. 'Have a table and some chairs brought here for when I call. It really is wonderful here. Here I shall read you... Goethe's *Faust*... that's what I shall read you.'

'Yes, there are no flies here,' she remarked artlessly. 'And when will you call?'

'The day after tomorrow.'

'Alright,' she said, 'I'll give orders.'

Natasha, who had entered the house together with us, suddenly shrieked and leapt back, all pale.

'What's the matter?' asked Vera Nikolayevna.

'Oh, Mama,' said the little girl, pointing into the corner, 'look what a horrible spider!…'

Vera Nikolayevna glanced into the corner: a large, striped spider was quietly crawling up the wall.

'What is there to be afraid of here?' she said. 'He doesn't bite, look.'

And before I could stop her, she had picked the ugly insect up, let it run about on her palm and tossed it away.

'Well, how brave you are!' I exclaimed.

'Where's the bravery in that? This spider isn't a poisonous one.'

'You're evidently strong on natural history, like before; whereas I wouldn't have picked it up.'

'There's no reason to be afraid of him,' repeated Vera Nikolayevna.

Natasha looked at us both in silence, and grinned.

'How like your mother she is!' I remarked.

'Yes,' said Vera Nikolayevna, with a smile of pleasure, 'I'm very glad about that. God grant she resemble her not in looks alone!'

We were called in to lunch, and after lunch I left. NB The lunch was very nice and tasty – I'm noting that in brackets for you, you glutton! Tomorrow I shall take them *Faust*. I'm afraid the old man Goethe and I might turn out a failure. I'll describe everything for you in detail.

Well, and what do you think now about all 'the events herein'? Probably… that she's had a powerful effect on me, that I'm ready to fall in love etc.? Nonsense, old fellow! It's time to move on. I've fooled around enough, that's it! You can't start life afresh at my age. And what's more, it wasn't women like that I fancied even before… But then what women did I fancy!!

I start to shudder – and my heart aches –
My idols make me feel ashamed. [10]

In any event, I'm very glad we are neighbours, glad of the opportunity to see an intelligent, straightforward, bright creature; and what will happen next, that you'll learn all in good time.

Your P.B.

FOURTH LETTER

THE VILLAGE OF M***OYE, 20TH JUNE 1850

The reading took place yesterday, my dear friend, and as to precisely how, the following points refer. First of all I should say: an unexpected success – though 'success' just isn't the word… Well, listen. I arrived for lunch. There were six of us at the table: her, Priyimkov, the daughter, the governess (an insignificant little white figure), me, and some old German in a short brown tailcoat, clean, shaved, scrubbed, with the most submissive and honest face, with a toothless smile and the smell of chicory coffee… all old Germans smell like that. We were introduced: this was a certain Schimmel, a German teacher from Priyimkov's neighbours, the Princes Kh***. It seems that Vera Nikolayevna is well disposed towards him and invited him to be present at the reading. We had a late lunch and did not leave the table for a long time, then we took a walk. The weather was wonderful. It was raining in the morning and there was a noisy wind, but everything had quietened down by the evening. She and I came out onto an open glade together. A large pink cloud hung high and light directly above the glade; streaks of grey stretched across it like smoke; at its very edge, now showing, now disappearing, there trembled a tiny star, while a little further off could be seen the white sickle of the moon against the azure sky, lightly tinged with scarlet. I pointed this cloud out to Vera Nikolayevna.

'Yes,' she said, 'it's beautiful, but just look over here.'

I looked around. A huge dark-blue storm cloud was rising up and blotting out the setting sun; in appearance it had the likeness of a fire-breathing mountain; its summit was thrown out across the sky in a broad cone; it was vividly edged all round with an ominous crimson glow which at one point, in the very centre, was breaking right through its heavy bulk, as though ripping itself out from a red-hot crater…

'Storm coming,' remarked Priyimkov.

But I'm digressing from the main item. In my last letter I forgot to tell you that when I got home from the Priyimkovs' I repented of having specified *Faust*; Schiller would have suited much better for the first occasion, if we had to be dealing with the Germans. I was particularly worried about the first scenes before the meeting with Gretchen; as regards Mephistopheles I wasn't untroubled either. But I was under the influence of *Faust* and could not willingly have read anything else. When it had already grown completely dark, we set off for the Chinese summer-house; it had been put in order the day before. Directly opposite the door, in front of a small sofa, stood a circular table covered with a rug; armchairs and chairs were set out all around; on the table a lamp was burning. I sat down on the sofa and took out the book. Vera Nikolayevna took a seat in an armchair some distance away, not far from the door. Beyond the door, in the midst of the darkness, a green acacia branch stood out, rocking slightly, lit up by the lamp; a current of night air would occasionally flow into the room. Priyimkov sat down near me by the table, the German next to him. The governess had stayed in the house with Natasha. I made a short introductory speech: I mentioned the ancient legend of Dr Faustus, the significance of Mephistopheles, Goethe himself, and I asked to be stopped if anything should seem obscure. Then I cleared my throat... Priyimkov asked me whether I needed some sugared water, and all the signs were there that he was very pleased with himself for putting this question to me. I refused. A deep silence fell. I began to read, without raising my eyes; I felt uncomfortable, my heart was pounding and my voice was shaking. The first exclamation of sympathy came from the German, and while the reading continued, he alone would break the silence... 'Astonishing! Sublime!' he repeated, occasionally adding: 'Now that is profound.' Priyimkov, so far as I could make out, was bored: he did not understand German very well and confessed himself that he did not like poetry!... But it was up to him! While sitting at the table, I had almost tried to hint that the reading could manage without him, but had felt ashamed to do so. Vera Nikolayevna did not stir; I stole a couple of glances at her: her eyes were fixed directly and attentively upon me; her face seemed pale to me. After Faust's first meeting with Gretchen she moved forward from the back of her armchair, folded her arms and remained motionless in that position until the end. I sensed that Priyimkov was having a wretched time of it, and this at first turned me cold, but little by little I forgot about him, became excited and read with fervour, with passion... I was reading for Vera Nikolayevna alone: an inner voice told me that *Faust* was having an effect on her. When I finished – I omitted the Intermezzo: that bit already belongs in manner to the second part; and I tossed out part of 'The Night Upon the Brocken' too – when I finished, when that last 'Heinrich!' had rung out, the German pronounced with emotion: 'God! How beautiful!' Priyimkov, as if gladdened (the poor man!), jumped up, sighed and began thanking me for the pleasure I had given... But I did not reply to him: I was gazing at Vera Nikolayevna... I wanted to hear what she would say. She got up, took some indecisive steps towards the door, stood for a while on the threshold and quietly went out into the garden. I hurried after her. She had already managed to move several steps away; the whiteness of her dress could just be seen in the dense shadow.

'Well then,' I cried, 'didn't you enjoy it?'

She stopped.

'Can you leave that book with me?' her voice rang out.

'I'll give it to you as a gift, Vera Nikolayevna, if you wish to have it.'

'I'm grateful!' she replied, and disappeared.

Priyimkov and the German came up to me.

'How amazingly warm!' remarked Priyimkov. 'Airless even. But where has my wife gone?'

'Home, it appears,' I replied.

'I think so, it'll soon be time for dinner,' he said. 'You read superbly,' he added, after a slight pause.

'Vera Nikolayevna appears to have enjoyed *Faust*,' I said.

'Without doubt!' exclaimed Priyimkov.

'Oh, but of course!' Schimmel joined in.

We arrived at the house.

'Where's the mistress?' enquired Priyimkov of a maid who was coming towards us.

'She's gone to her bedroom.'

Priyimkov went off to the bedroom.

I went out onto the terrace along with Schimmel. The old man raised his eyes to the sky.

'How many stars!' he said slowly, after taking some snuff. 'And they're all worlds,' he added, before sniffing a second time.

I did not think it necessary to answer him and only looked up in silence. A secret perplexity weighed upon my soul. The stars seemed to me to be looking at us seriously. After five minutes or so Priyimkov appeared and called us into the dining-room. Soon Vera Nikolayevna came in too. We sat down.

'Just look at Verochka,' said Priyimkov to me.

I glanced at her.

'What? Don't you notice anything?'

I did indeed notice a change in her face, but I replied, I don't know why: 'No, nothing.'

'Her eyes are red,' continued Priyimkov.

I remained silent.

'Just imagine, I've gone upstairs to her room, and I find her crying. It's a long time since that's happened with her. I can tell you when the last time she cried was: when our Sasha passed away. There's what you've done with your *Faust*!' he added, with a smile.

'So now, Vera Nikolayevna,' I began, 'you can see that I was right when…'

'I didn't expect this,' she interrupted me, 'but still God knows whether you're right. Perhaps Mother forbade me to read such books for the very reason that she knew…'

Vera Nikolayevna stopped.

'That she knew?' I repeated. 'Go on.'

'To what end? I'm ashamed as it is: what was it I was crying about? But then you and I will discuss it further. There was a lot I didn't understand at all.'

'Why didn't you stop me then?'

'I understood all the words and their meaning, but…'

She did not finish what she was saying and fell into thought. At that instant from the garden there came a rustling of leaves suddenly shaken by the rising wind. Vera Nikolayevna winced and turned to face the wide-open window.

'I told you there'd be a storm!' exclaimed Priyimkov. 'But Verochka, why is it you're wincing like that?'

She glanced at him in silence. A weak flash of distant lightning was reflected mysteriously on her immobile face.

'All thanks to *Faust*,' continued Priyimkov. 'After dinner it'll have to be straight to bed... isn't that so, Mr Schimmel?'

'After moral pleasure physical rest is just as beneficial as it is health-giving,' said the kind German, and drank down a glass of vodka.

We dispersed immediately after dinner. Saying goodnight to Vera Nikolayevna I shook her hand: it was cold. I went to the room that I had been given and stood for a long time at the window before undressing and getting into bed. Priyimkov's prediction came true: the storm approached and broke out. I listened to the noise of the wind, the knocking and slapping of the rain, watched as, with every flash of lightning, the church, built nearby above the lake, would be now suddenly black against a white background, now white against black, now swallowed up by the gloom once again... But my thoughts were far away. I was thinking of Vera Nikolayevna, thinking of what she would say to me when she had read *Faust* for herself, thinking of her tears, recalling how she had listened...

The storm had already passed long ago – the stars had begun to shine, everything had fallen quiet all around. Some bird unknown to me was singing in different voices, repeating one and the same figure several times in succession. Its resonant, solitary voice sounded strange in the midst of the profound silence; and still I did not go to bed...

The next morning I went down into the drawing-room earlier than anyone, and stopped in front of the portrait of Yeltsova. 'Well, you've got to accept it,' I thought, with a secret feeling of mocking triumph, 'you see, I've read your daughter a forbidden book!' Suddenly I imagined... you've probably noticed that eyes *en face* always seem to be directed straight at the viewer... but on this occasion I really did imagine that the old woman had trained them on me in reproach.

I turned away, went up to the window, and saw Vera Nikolayevna. With an umbrella on her shoulder, with a light white scarf on her head, she was walking through the garden. I immediately went out of the house and greeted her.

'I've been awake all night,' she told me, 'I've got a headache; I came out into the air – perhaps it will pass.'

'Surely it's not because of yesterday's reading?' I asked.

'Of course: I'm not used to it. In that book of yours there are things I simply can't escape from; I think they're what is burning my head so,' she added, putting her hand to her forehead.

'That's splendid,' I said, 'but this is the bad part: I'm afraid this insomnia and headache might dispel your desire to read such things.'

'Do you think so?' she said, and, in passing, broke off a wild jasmine twig. 'God knows! It seems to me that anyone who once steps onto this road will never turn back.'

Suddenly she threw the twig aside.

'Let's go and sit down in this gazebo,' she continued, 'and please, until I myself begin to talk with you, don't mention... that book to me.' (It was as if she were afraid to pronounce the name *Faust*.)

We went into the gazebo and sat down.

'I shan't talk to you about *Faust*,' I began, 'but you'll allow me to congratulate you and tell you that I envy you.'

'You envy me?'

'Yes; with your soul, as I now know you, how much enjoyment you have ahead of you! There are great poets besides Goethe: Shakespeare, Schiller, and our own Pushkin too... you must get to know him as well.'

She was silent and drew lines in the sand with the umbrella.

Oh my friend, Semyon Nikolayich, if you could have seen how pretty she was at that moment: pale almost to the point of transparency, bending slightly, tired, inwardly disturbed – and nonetheless clear as the sky! I talked, talked for a long time, then fell quiet – and sat like that, silently gazing at her...

She did not raise her eyes, and continued either drawing with the umbrella or rubbing out what she had drawn. Suddenly the nimble steps of a child were heard: Natasha ran into the gazebo. Vera Nikolayevna straightened up, rose and, to my surprise, embraced her daughter with a kind of impetuous tenderness... That is not her way. Then Priyimkov appeared. The grey-haired but tidy-minded baby Schimmel had left before first light so as not to miss a lesson. We went to drink tea.

However, I'm tired; it's time to finish this letter. It must seem to you nonsensical, confused. I feel confused myself. I'm not myself. I don't know what's wrong with me. I keep on imagining a small room with bare walls, a lamp, a wide-open door; the scent and freshness of the night, and there, beside the door, an attentive young face, light, white clothes… I understand now why I wanted to marry her: evidently I wasn't as stupid before the trip to Berlin as I'd thought up until now. Yes, Semyon Nikolayich, your friend finds himself in a strange spiritual state. All this will pass, I know… and if it doesn't pass – well, what of it? – it doesn't pass. But all the same I'm pleased with myself: firstly, I spent an astounding evening; and secondly, if I have awakened this spirit, who can blame me? The old woman, Yeltsova, is nailed to the wall and has to remain silent. The old woman!… The details of her life are not all known to me, but I do know that she ran away from her father's home – not for nothing, evidently, was she born of an Italian mother. She wanted insurance for her daughter… We'll see.

I'm throwing down the pen. Please think whatever you like of me, you sardonic man, but don't mock me in writing. You and I are old friends and ought to spare one another. Goodbye!

Your P.B.

FIFTH LETTER

THE VILLAGE OF M***OYE, 26TH JULY 1850

I've not written to you for a long time, dear Semyon Nikolayich, for more than a month, I think. There have been things to write about, but idleness got the better of me. To tell the truth, I've hardly thought about you all this time. But I can conclude from your last letter to me that you are making assumptions about me that are unjust, that is, not entirely just. You think I am captivated by Vera (I feel awkward somehow calling her Vera Nikolayevna); you're mistaken. Of course, I see her often, I am extremely fond of her... but who wouldn't be fond of her? I'd like to see you in my place. An amazing creature! Instant perspicacity alongside the innocence of a child, clear common sense and an innate feeling for beauty, constant aspiration towards truth, towards the elevated, and understanding of everything, even vice, even the ridiculous – and above all this, like the white wings of an angel, such feminine charm... Well it can't be denied! She and I have read a lot, talked a lot during this month. Reading with her is a pleasure such as I have never before experienced. It's as if you're discovering new countries. She does not go into raptures about anything: all noise is alien to her; she is all quietly aglow when she likes something, and her face adopts an expression of such nobility and goodness... specifically goodness. From her earliest childhood Vera has not known what a lie is: she has become accustomed to the truth, she breathes it, and for that reason truth alone seems natural to her in poetry too; she recognises it immediately, without difficulty or strain, like a familiar face... a great advantage and good fortune! One cannot but think well of her mother for that. How many times have I thought, looking at Vera: yes, Goethe is right:

> *A good man in his unclear aspiration*
> *Is fully conscious where the true path lies.*[11]

One thing is annoying: her husband keeps hanging around. (Please don't laugh a stupid laugh, don't profane our pure friendship even in

25

thought.) He is just as capable of understanding poetry as I am disposed to play the flute, but he does not want to fall behind his wife, he wants to be enlightened as well. Sometimes she exasperates me herself; some mood will suddenly come upon her: she doesn't want to read or talk, works at her tambour, spends time with Natasha, with the housekeeper, runs all of a sudden to the kitchen, or simply sits with her arms tightly crossed and keeps looking out of the window, or else starts playing old maid with the nanny... I've noticed that in these instances she shouldn't be bothered, it's better to wait for her to come to you herself, to start a conversation or to pick up a book. There is a great deal of independence in her, and I'm very glad of it. Sometimes, you remember, in the days of our youth, some girl would repeat to you as best she could your very own words, and you'd get carried away by this echo and perhaps worship it, until you got to the bottom of what was going on; but this one... no: this one goes her own way. She won't take anything on trust; you won't intimidate her with authority; she won't think of arguing, but neither will she yield. She and I have discussed *Faust* on more than one occasion: yet – it's a strange thing! – she says nothing herself about Gretchen, but only listens to what I'll say to her. Mephistopheles frightens her not as a devil, but as 'something that might be found in anyone'... Those are her own words. I began to explain to her that we call this 'something' reflection; but she didn't understand the word reflection in the German sense: she only knows the French *réflexion* and is accustomed to thinking it beneficial. Our relationship is astonishing! From a certain point of view I can say that I have a great influence on her and am, as it were, educating her; but she too, without noticing it herself, is in many respects changing me for the better. Only thanks to her, for example, have I recently discovered what a huge amount of the conventional, the rhetorical there is in many fine and well-known poetic works. What she remains cold towards is, in my eyes, already under suspicion. Yes, I've become better, clearer. To be near her, to meet with her and remain the person you used to be is impossible.

What emerges from all this then? you'll ask. And I really do think – nothing. I shall spend the time until September most pleasantly, and then I shall leave. Life will seem dark and dull to me in the first months… I'll get used to it. I know how dangerous any sort of liaison is between a man and a young woman, how one feeling is replaced, unnoticed, by another… I would be able to break away, if I were not conscious that we are both perfectly calm. Once, it's true, something strange happened between us. I don't know how and in consequence of what – I seem to recall we were reading *Onegin*[12] – but I kissed her hand. She moved away a little, fastened her gaze upon me (I've not seen such a gaze in anyone but her: there is pensiveness in it, and attention, and a sort of severity)… suddenly she blushed, got up, and left. I didn't manage to be alone with her again that day. She avoided me and for a good four hours played her card-games with her husband, the nanny and the governess! The next morning she invited me to go into the garden. We walked all the way through it to the lake. Without turning towards me, she suddenly whispered quietly: 'Please, don't do that in future!' and immediately began telling me something… I felt very shamed.

I must admit that her image does not leave my mind, and I began writing this letter to you with little more intention than having the opportunity to think and talk about her. I can hear the snorting of horses and the clatter of their hooves: it's my carriage that's been made ready. I'm going to see them. My coachman no longer asks me where to drive now when I get into the carriage – he takes me straight to the Priyimkovs'. Two kilometres before you reach their village, on a sharp bend in the road, their house suddenly peeps out from behind a birch grove… My heart fills with joy every time, just as soon as her windows sparkle in the distance. Schimmel (that harmless old man occasionally visits them; the Princes Kh*** they have seen, thank God, only once)… not for nothing does Schimmel say with his characteristically modest solemnity, indicating the house where Vera lives: 'That is the abode of peace!' An angel of peace certainly has taken up residence in that house…

So cloak me with your wing and calm
The agitation of my breast –
The shade will be as healing balm
And set my captive soul at rest…[13]

27

But enough, however; otherwise God knows what you'll think. Until the next time... Whatever will I write the next time? Goodbye! Incidentally, she'll never say: 'goodbye', but always: 'well, goodbye'. I'm terribly fond of that.

Your P.B.

PS I don't know whether I ever told you that she knows I asked to marry her.

SIXTH LETTER

THE VILLAGE OF M***OYE, 10TH AUGUST 1850

Admit it, you expect a letter from me that is either despairing or rapturous… Nothing of the sort! My letter will be like all the others. Nothing new has happened, nor does it seem it can happen. A few days ago we went out boating on the lake. I'll describe the trip for you. There were three of us: her, Schimmel and me. I don't understand what makes her invite that old man so often. The Kh*** family are grumbling about him, saying he has started to neglect his lessons. But then on this occasion he was amusing. Priyimkov didn't go with us: he had a head-ache. The weather was splendid, cheerful: big white clouds, looking as if they'd been ripped apart across the blue sky, brilliance everywhere, a rustling in the trees, the splashing and slapping of the water by the shore, fleeting golden ripples on the waves, fresh air and sunshine! At first the German and I rowed; then we raised the sail and sped away. The bow of the boat really started diving, and behind the stern the wake hissed and foamed. She sat down at the rudder and began to steer; she had tied a scarf on her head: a hat would have been carried away; her curls were torn out from beneath it and beat softly at the air. She held the rudder firmly with her tanned little hand, and smiled at the spray that occasionally flew into her face. I curled up in the bottom of the boat, not far from her feet; the German took out his pipe, lit up his tobacco and – just imagine – began singing in quite a pleasant bass voice. First he sang the old song '*Freu't euch des Lebens*'[14], then an aria from *The Magic Flute*, then a romance by the name of 'The Alphabet of Love' – '*Das A-B-C der Liebe*'. This song goes – with decent comic verses, naturally – through the whole alphabet, beginning with 'A, B, C, D – When you I see!' and ending with 'W, X, Y, Z – Bow down your head'. He sang all the couplets through with a sensitive expression; but it had to be seen, the way he roguishly screwed up his left eye at the word: 'head'. Vera burst out laughing and wagged her finger at him. I remarked that, so far as I could tell, Mr Schimmel was nobody's fool in his day. 'Quite right, and I could stick up for myself!' he said

29

pompously, knocked the ash from the pipe out onto his palm and, dipping his fingers into his tobacco-pouch rakishly from the side, bit on the mouthpiece of his pipe-stem. 'When I was a student,' he added, 'oh-ho-ho!' He said nothing more. But what an 'oh-ho-ho' it was! Vera asked him to sing a student song of some sort, and he sang her '*Knaster, den gelben*'[15], but the last note was out of tune. He really had got quite carried away. Meanwhile the wind had strengthened, quite big waves had started to roll, the boat was tilting slightly, swallows had begun darting low around us. We reset the sail and started tacking. The wind suddenly shifted, we didn't have time to right ourselves – a wave splashed over the side, the boat became very waterlogged. And at this point the German showed his mettle; he tore the rope away from me and set the sail properly, saying as he did so: 'This is how it's done in Cuxhaven!' – '*So macht man's in Cuxhaven!*'

Vera was probably frightened, because she turned pale, but, as is her wont, did not utter a word, gathered up her dress and put the tips of her feet on the boat's transom. A poem by Goethe suddenly came into my head (for some time I've been absolutely plagued by him)… do you remember: 'On the waters glitter a thousand rocking stars'[16], and I recited it loudly. When I reached the line: 'Eyes, my eyes, why sink you down?' she raised her eyes a little (I was sitting lower than her: her gaze fell on me from above) and looked into the distance for a long time, squinting because of the wind… Light rain was upon us in a moment and bubbles began to jump across the water. I offered her my coat: she threw it over her shoulders. We put in to the shore – not at the landing-stage – and reached the house on foot. I led her by the arm. It was as if I constantly wanted to say something to her; but I was silent. I seem to recall, however, that I did ask her why she always sat beneath Mrs Yeltsova's portrait when she was at home, like a fledgling under its mother's wing. 'Your simile is very apt,' she said, 'I should never wish to come out from under her wing.' 'Would not wish to come out and be at liberty?' I asked again. She made no reply.

I don't know why I've recounted this outing to you – perhaps just because it has remained in my memory as one of the brightest events of the past days, although in reality what kind of event is it? I was so gratified and wordlessly cheerful, and tears, easy and happy tears were just begging to be shed.

Yes! Imagine, the next day, passing by a gazebo in the garden, I suddenly hear someone's pleasant, resonant, female voice: it's singing: '*Freu't euch des Lebens…*' I glanced into the gazebo: it was Vera. 'Bravo!' I exclaimed, 'I didn't even know you had such a splendid voice!' She became embarrassed and fell silent. Joking apart, she has an excellent, powerful soprano. Yet I don't think she even suspected she had a good voice. How many untouched riches are still hidden within her! She does not know herself. But isn't it true, that such a woman is a rarity nowadays?

We had the strangest conversation yesterday. First we talked about ghosts. Imagine: she believes in them and says she has her reasons for this. Priyimkov, who was sitting there too, lowered his eyes and shook his head as if in confirmation of her words. I started questioning her, but soon noticed that she found this conversation unpleasant. We began to talk about the imagination, about the power of the imagination. I told how in my youth, when I dreamt about happiness a lot (a common pastime for people who have not been, or are not lucky in life), I dreamt among other things of what bliss it would be to spend several weeks in Venice together with a woman I loved. I thought about this so often, especially in the nights, that little by little a whole picture formed in my head, which I could call up before me at will: I had only to close my eyes. This is what I imagined: night-time, the moon, the light from the moon, white and gentle, the scent… you're thinking 'of lemon'? no, of vanilla, the scent of cactus, a broad expanse of smooth water, a flat island overgrown with olive trees; on the island, right by the shore's edge, a small marble house with wide-open windows; music can be heard, God knows from where; in the house are trees with dark leaves and the light of a half-shaded lamp; a heavy velvet mantle with a gold fringe has been draped out of one window and has one end lying on the water; and *he* and *she* are sitting next to one another, leaning on the mantle, gazing into the distance to where Venice can be seen. I could imagine all this so clearly, as though I had seen it all with my own eyes. She heard out my fantasies and said that she too often dreamed,

31

but that her dreams were of a different kind: she either imagined herself on the plains of Africa with some traveller, or seeking out the trail of Franklin[17] in the Arctic Ocean; she could vividly imagine all the deprivations she must suffer, all the difficulties with which she would be obliged to struggle...

'You've read too many travel books,' remarked her husband.

'Perhaps,' she said, 'but if you have to dream, who wants to dream about the unattainable?'

'But why not?' I joined in. 'What has the poor old unattainable done wrong?'

'I expressed myself wrongly,' she said, 'what I meant was: who wants to dream about himself, about his own happiness? There's no point in thinking about it; if it doesn't appear, why chase after it? It's like good health: when you don't notice it, that means it's there.'

These words surprised me. Within this woman is a great spirit, believe me... From Venice the conversation moved on to Italy, to the Italians. Priyimkov left the room, Vera and I remained alone.

'In your veins too there flows Italian blood,' I remarked.

'Yes,' she said, 'would you like me to show you a portrait of my grandmother?'

'If you'd be so kind.'

She went to her study and from there she brought quite a large gold locket. Opening this locket, I saw superbly painted miniature portraits of Yeltsova's father and his wife – this peasant woman from Albano. Vera's grandfather struck me by his similarity to his daughter. Only his features, fringed with a white cloud of powder, seemed even more severe, pointed and sharp, while in his little yellow eyes there shone a certain sullen obstinacy. But what a face the Italian had! Voluptuous, open, like a rose in full bloom, with large, moist, prominent eyes and rosy lips, smiling in self-satisfaction! The fine, sensual nostrils seemed to be quivering and dilating as after recent kisses; the dark-complexioned cheeks positively radiated sultry good health, the luxuriance of youth and feminine strength... That brow had never reasoned, and thank God for it! She was drawn in her Albano costume; the painter (a master!) had placed a vine twig in her hair, black as pitch, with bright grey highlights: this Bacchic adornment could not have been better suited to the expression on her face. And do you know who I was reminded of by this face? My Manon Lescaut in the black frame. And what is most surprising of all: looking at this portrait I remembered that, despite the utter dissimilarity of outlines, in Vera there is at times a glimpse of something resembling this smile, this look...

Yes, I repeat: neither she herself, nor anybody else on earth yet knows all that is hidden inside her...

Incidentally! Just before her daughter's wedding Yeltsova related the whole of her life to her, the death of her own mother etc., probably with an instructive aim. Vera was particularly affected by what she heard about her grandfather, about this mysterious Ladanov. Is it perhaps because of this that she believes in ghosts? It's strange! She is herself so pure and bright, yet she fears everything that is gloomy, of the netherworld, and she believes in it...

However, enough. Why write all this? But then, since it's already been written, let it be sent off to you too.

Your P.B.

SEVENTH LETTER

From the same to the same

I take up my pen ten days after the last letter... Oh my friend, I can conceal myself no more... How wretched I am! How I love her! You can imagine with what a bitter shudder I write that fateful word. I am not a boy, not even a young man; I am no longer of an age when deceiving another is almost impossible, while deceiving oneself costs nothing. I know everything and can see clearly. I know that I'm almost forty, that she is the wife of another man, that she loves her husband; I know very well that from the unfortunate feeling that has taken possession of me I can expect nothing other than secret torments and the final squandering of my life forces – I know all of this, I hope for nothing and want nothing; but this does not make things any easier. About a month ago I had already begun to notice that the attraction she held for me was becoming stronger and stronger. This in part embarrassed, in part even pleased me... Yet could I have expected that things, for which, just like youth, there had seemed to be no return, would all be repeated for me? But what am I saying! I never loved like this, no, never! Manon Lescauts, Fretillons[18] – these were my idols. Such idols are easily smashed; but now... only now have I learnt what it means to fall in love with a woman. I feel ashamed even to talk about it; but it is so. I feel ashamed... Love is, after all, egotism; and to be an egotist at my age is impermissible: you cannot live for yourself at thirty-seven; you should live usefully, with a purpose on earth, carry out your duty, your task. And I had begun to take up work... And again everything has been scattered, as if by a whirlwind! Now I understand what I was writing to you about in my first letter; I understand what test I was lacking. How suddenly this blow has fallen on my head! I am standing and gazing senselessly ahead: a black curtain hangs just in front of my eyes; my soul is wretched and fearful! I can restrain myself, I am outwardly calm, not only for others, even in private; I can't rave, after all, as if I really were a boy! But the worm has crawled into my heart and is sucking at it day and night. How will it end? Until now I had pined and fretted in her absence, and calmed down immediately in her presence... Now I am troubled in her presence – that is what frightens me. Oh my friend, how hard it is to be ashamed of one's tears, to conceal them!... Youth alone can be permitted to cry; it alone is suited by tears...

I cannot reread this letter; it has been torn from me involuntarily, like a groan. I cannot add anything, relate anything... Give me time: I'll come to my senses, take a hold on my soul, I'll speak to you like a man, but now I should like to lean my head on your breast and...

O, Mephistopheles! You too fail to help me. I stopped on purpose, on purpose I tried to rouse the ironic vein within me, to remind myself of how ridiculous and sickly these complaints, these outpourings would seem to me in a year, in six months... No, Mephistopheles is powerless, and his tooth is blunt... Goodbye.

Your P.B.

EIGHTH LETTER

From the same to the same

My dear friend, Semyon Nikolayich!

You took my last letter too much to heart. You know how I'm always inclined to exaggerate my sensations. It happens involuntarily somehow with me: a woman's nature! It will, of course, pass with the years; but I admit with a sigh, I have still not reformed as yet. And so relax. I will not deny the impression made on me by Vera, but then again I'll say there is nothing unusual in all this. There is no need at all for you to come here, as you write. To gallop a thousand kilometres because of God knows what – that would be simply madness! But I am very grateful to you for this new proof of your friendship and, believe me, shall never forget it. Your journey here is also inappropriate because I myself intend to leave soon for St Petersburg. Sitting on your sofa I shall tell you many things, whereas now I really don't feel like it: who knows, I might talk too much again and confuse things. Before I leave I'll write to you once more. And so until we meet again soon, be well and happy, and don't grieve too much over the lot – of

Your devoted P.B.

NINTH LETTER

THE VILLAGE OF P***OYE, 10TH MARCH 1853

I did not reply to your letter for a long time; I have been thinking about it all these days. I felt that it was prompted in you not by idle curiosity, but by true friendly concern; yet I nonetheless wavered: should I follow your advice, should I carry out your wish? Finally I made up my mind; I shall tell you everything. Whether my confession will relieve me, as you suppose, I don't know; but it seems to me that I have no right to conceal from you the thing that changed my life for ever; it seems to me that I would even be at fault... alas! even more at fault before that unforgettable, dear shade, if I did not entrust our sad secret to the only heart I still hold dear. Perhaps you alone on earth remember about Vera, and you make flippant and false judgements about her; that I cannot allow. And so learn everything. Alas! It can all be conveyed in two words. What there was between us flashed by in an instant like lightning, and, like lightning, brought death and ruin...

More than two years have gone by since she passed away, since I settled here in this backwater, which I shall not now leave until the end of my days, and yet everything is so clear in my memory, my wounds are still so raw, my grief so bitter...

I shall not be complaining. Complaints, in irritating, alleviate sorrow, but not mine. I shall be recounting.

You remember my last letter – that letter in which I thought to dispel your fears and advised against your setting out from St Petersburg? You were suspicious of its forced nonchalance, you did not believe we would meet again soon: you were right. On the eve of that day when I wrote to you, I learnt that I was loved.

Tracing these words, I have realised how difficult it will be for me to continue my story to the end. The persistent thought of her death will torment me with redoubled force, I shall be seared by these memories... But I shall try to control myself and will either give up writing or not say an unnecessary word.

This is how I learnt that Vera loved me. First of all I should tell you (and you will believe me) that until that day I suspected absolutely nothing. True, she had started sometimes falling into a reverie, which had never been the case with her previously, but I did not understand why this was happening to her. Finally, one day, on the 7th of September – a notable day for me – this is what happened. You know how I loved her and how wretched I was. I wandered about like a shadow, I couldn't keep still. I meant to stay at home, but couldn't bear it and set off to see her. I found her alone in her study. Priyimkov was not at home: he had gone off hunting. When I went in to Vera she looked at me intently and did not reply to my bow. She was sitting by the window; on her knees lay a book which I recognised immediately: it was my *Faust*. Her face expressed fatigue. I sat down opposite her. She asked me to read out loud the scene between Faust and Gretchen where she asks him whether he believes in God. I took the book and began to read. When I had finished, I glanced at her. With her head leaning against the back of the armchair and her arms crossed on her breast, she was still looking at me just as intently.

I don't know why my heart suddenly began pounding.

'What have you done to me!' she said in a slow voice.

'What?' I asked in confusion.

'Yes, what have you done to me!' she repeated.

'Do you mean,' I began, 'why did I persuade you to read such books?'

She stood up in silence and went to leave the room. I gazed after her. On the threshold she stopped and turned back to me.

'I love you,' she said, 'that's what you've done to me.'

The blood rushed to my head...

'I love you, I'm in love with you,' repeated Vera.

She left and closed the door behind her. I will not begin to describe to you what happened to me then. I remember I went out into the garden, made my way into its depths, leant up against a tree, and how long I spent standing there, I cannot say. It was as if I had frozen; every so often a feeling of bliss ran in waves through my heart... No, I won't begin to speak about that. I was summoned from my numbed state by Priyimkov's voice; someone had been sent to tell him that I had arrived: he had returned from the hunt and was looking for me. He was astonished to find me alone in the garden, hatless, and he led me into the house. 'My wife's in the drawing-room,' he said, 'let's go and join her.' You can imagine the feelings with which I crossed the threshold of the drawing-room. Vera was sitting in the corner at her tambour; I stole a glance at her and did not raise my eyes for a long time afterwards. To my surprise, she appeared calm – in what she said, in the sound of her voice, no alarm could be heard. Finally I made up my mind to look at her. Our eyes met. She flushed slightly and bent over her canvas. I began observing her. She seemed to be bewildered; a mirthless smile occasionally touched her lips.

Priyimkov left the room. She suddenly raised her head and asked me quite loudly:

'What do you intend to do now?'

I became confused and hurriedly replied in a hollow voice that I intended to fulfil the duty of an honest man and withdraw, 'because,' I added, 'I love you, Vera Nikolayevna, you probably noticed that long ago.' She again bent down towards the canvas and fell into thought.

'I must have a talk with you,' she said. 'Come this evening after tea to our summer-house... you know, where you read *Faust*.'

She said this so distinctly that even now I cannot comprehend how Priyimkov, who was entering the room at that very instant, did not hear anything. That day passed quietly, agonisingly quietly. Vera sometimes gazed around with such an expression, as if she were wondering whether she was dreaming. And at the same time resolve was written on her face. While I... I could not come to my senses. Vera loves me! These words were continually turning round in my mind; but I did not understand them – I did not understand either myself, or her. I did not believe such unexpected, such staggering good fortune; it took an effort to recall what had passed, and I too gazed and spoke as though in a dream...

After tea, when I was already beginning to think how I might slip out of the house unnoticed, she herself suddenly announced that she wanted to go for a walk and suggested I accompany her. I rose, picked up my hat and set off to follow her. I did not dare to begin speaking, I was scarcely breathing, I was waiting for the first word from her, waiting for confessions; but she was silent. We reached the Chinese summer-house in silence, we entered it in silence, and here – I still don't know, can't understand how it happened – we suddenly found ourselves in one another's arms. Some unseen force had thrown me towards her and her towards me. In the dying light of the day her face, with its curls tossed back, lit up for a moment with a smile of abandon and languor, and our lips merged in a kiss…

That kiss was our first and our last.

Vera suddenly tore herself out of my arms and, with an expression of horror in her widened eyes, she reeled back from me…

'Look behind you,' she said to me, her voice trembling, 'do you see anything?'

I turned around quickly.

'No, nothing. Can you see something then?'

'I can't now, but I did see something.'

She was breathing deeply and slowly.

'Whom? What?'

'My mother,' she said slowly, and her whole body began to tremble.

I shivered as well, as though I had come over cold; I suddenly felt awful, like a criminal. And was I not indeed a criminal at that moment?

'Enough!' I began, 'what is all this? Tell me instead…'

'No, for God's sake, no!' she interrupted, and took her head in her hands. 'It's madness… I'm going mad… This is no joking matter – this is death… Goodbye…'

I reached out my arms to her.

'Stop, for God's sake, for a moment,' I exclaimed in an involuntary rush. I didn't know what to say and could hardly stay on my feet. 'For God's sake… I mean, this is cruel.'

She glanced at me.

'Tomorrow, tomorrow evening,' she said, 'not today, I beg you… leave today… tomorrow evening come to the garden gate beside the lake. I'll be there, I'll come… I swear to you, I'll come,' she added animatedly, and her eyes shone, 'whoever might try to stop me, I swear! I'll tell you everything, only let me go today.'

And before I could say a word, she had vanished.

Shaken to the core, I stayed where I was. My head was spinning. Through the mad joy that was filling my entire being there stole a feeling of melancholy… I looked around. The damp, God-forsaken room in which I stood seemed terrible to me with its low vault and its dark walls.

I went outside and directed my heavy steps towards the house. Vera was waiting for me on the terrace; she entered the house as soon as I came near and immediately withdrew to her bedroom.

I left.

How I spent the night and the following day until the evening – that cannot be conveyed. I only remember that I lay face down with my face hidden in my hands, recalling her smile before the kiss and whispering: 'There she is, at last…'

I also recalled the words of Yeltsova, conveyed to me by Vera. She had said to her one day: 'You're like ice: until you melt, you're strong as stone, but when you melt, not even a trace of you will be left.'

This is what else came to mind: Vera and I were once discussing what was meant by know-how, talent.

'I know how to do only one thing,' she said, 'remain silent until the last moment.'

At that time I understood nothing.

'But what does her fright mean?…' I wondered. 'Surely she didn't really see Yeltsova? Imagination!' I thought, and once more gave myself over to sensations of expectation.

That same day I wrote to you – with what ideas, I dread to recall – that sly letter.

In the evening – the sun was not yet setting – I was already standing some fifty paces from the garden gate among some tall, dense willows on the shore of the lake. I had come from home on foot. I confess, to my shame: fear, the most pusillanimous fear, filled my breast, I was constantly starting… but I did not feel repentant. Hidden among the branches I gazed persistently at the gate. It did not open. The sun had set, evening had approached; the stars had already come out, and the sky had turned black. Nobody appeared. I was wracked by fever. The night came on. I could bear it no longer. I cautiously emerged from the willows and stole up to the gate. All was quiet in the garden. I called to Vera in a whisper, called a second time, a third… No voice responded. Another half-hour passed, an hour passed; it became completely dark.

Waiting had exhausted me; I pulled the gate towards me, opened it at a stroke, and on tiptoe, like a thief, moved towards the house. I stopped in the shadow of the limes.

Almost all the windows in the house were lit up; people were going backwards and forwards through the rooms. This surprised me: my watch, so far as I could distinguish by the dim light of the stars, showed half past eleven. Suddenly, a clattering rang out beyond the house: a carriage was driving out of the courtyard.

'Guests, evidently,' I thought. Having lost all hope of seeing Vera, I made my way out of the garden and set off for home at a rapid pace. The September night was dark, but warm and windless. The feeling that had all but overwhelmed me, not so much of annoyance as of sadness, was gradually dispelled, and I arrived home a little tired from walking fast, but calmed by the silence of the night, happy and almost cheerful. I went into my bedroom, sent Timofei away, threw myself onto the bed without undressing, and sank into thought.

At first my dreams were comforting; but soon I noticed a strange change in myself. I began to feel some secret, gnawing anguish, some profound inner disquiet. I could not understand why this was happening; but I was starting to feel dread and weariness, as if threatened by misfortune close by, as if somebody dear were suffering at that moment and calling on me for help. On the table burned the small, still flame of a wax candle, the ticking of a pendulum was heavy and measured. I propped up my head with my hand and set about gazing into the empty semi-darkness of my lonely room. I thought of Vera, and inside me my soul began to ache: everything I had so rejoiced at now seemed to me, as, indeed, it ought to have done, misfortune, inescapable ruin. The feeling of anguish grew and grew within me, I could lie down no longer; I suddenly imagined once more that someone was calling me in an imploring voice... I raised my head a little and started; so it was, I wasn't deceiving myself: a pitiful cry sped to me from afar and clung, weakly tinkling, to the black panes of the window. I became terrified. I leapt up from the bed, opened the window wide. A distinct groan burst into the room and seemed to circle above me. Quite cold in horror, I heard its final, dying modulations. It seemed as if somebody were being cut open in the distance, and as if the unfortunate were begging in vain for mercy. Whether it was an owl that had cried out in the copse, or some other creature that had emitted this groan, I was not aware at the time, but, like Mazepa to Kochubei[19], I called out in reply to this ominous sound.

'Vera, Vera!' I exclaimed, 'is that you calling me?'

Timofei appeared before me, sleepy and bewildered.

I recovered myself, drank a glass of water, moved into another room; but sleep did not come to me. My heart was beating morbidly inside me, albeit not fast. I was no longer able to give myself over to dreams of happiness; I no longer dared believe in it.

The next day before lunch I set off to call on Priyimkov. He greeted me with a troubled face.

'My wife is ill,' he began, 'she's in bed; I've had the doctor here.'

'What's wrong with her?'

'I don't understand it. Yesterday evening she went out into the garden, then suddenly returned, beside herself with fright. The maid ran to fetch me. I go and ask my wife 'what's the matter with you?' She doesn't answer, but goes to bed straight away; during the night she became delirious. She was saying God knows what in her delirium, she mentioned you. The maid told me an astonishing thing: Verochka is supposed to have seen the ghost of her late mother in the garden, supposed to have had the impression that it was walking towards her with wide-open arms.'

You can imagine what I felt at these words.

'Of course it's nonsense,' continued Priyimkov, 'but I must admit that unusual things of this sort have happened with my wife.'

'And tell me, is Vera Nikolayevna very unwell?'

'Yes, she's unwell: things were bad in the night; now she's only half-conscious.'

'And what did the doctor say?'

'The doctor said the illness has not yet taken shape...'

12TH MARCH

I cannot continue in the way I began, dear friend: it costs me too great an effort and reopens my wounds too painfully. The illness, to use the words of the doctor, took shape, and Vera died of this illness. She did

43

not live even two weeks after the fateful day of our fleeting tryst. I saw her once more before her death. I have no memory more cruel. I already knew from the doctor that there was no hope. Late one evening, when everyone in the house had already gone to bed, I stole up to the doors of her bedroom and glanced into it. Vera lay on the bed with her eyes closed, thin, small, with a feverish flush on her cheeks. As if turned to stone I looked at her. Suddenly she opened her eyes wide, turned them on me, peered, and, reaching out an emaciated arm:

'What does he want in this holy place?
That man... him there...'[20]

– she pronounced in a voice so terrible that I fled headlong. Almost throughout her illness she raved about *Faust* and her mother, whom she sometimes called Martha, sometimes Gretchen's mother.

Vera died. I was at her funeral. Since then I have abandoned everything and settled here for good.

Now think about what I have told you; think about her, about this creature who died so soon. How it happened, how to interpret this incomprehensible interference of the dead in the affairs of the living, I do not know and shall never know; but you must agree that it was not a fit of capricious depression that made me withdraw from society. I have become a different man from the one you knew: I believe many things now that I did not believe before. All this time I have thought so much about that unfortunate woman (I almost said 'girl'), about her parentage, about the secret game of fate on which we, the blind, bestow the name of blind chance. Who knows how many seeds each person living on the earth leaves, which are fated to spring up only after his death? Who can say by what mysterious chain the fate of a man is linked with the fate of his children, his descendants, and how his aspirations affect them, how his mistakes are answered for by them? We must all submit and bow our heads before the Unknown.

Yes, Vera perished, while I survived. I remember, when I was still a child, we had in the house a beautiful vase of transparent alabaster. Not a single spot defiled its virginal whiteness. One day, left on my own, I began rocking the pedestal on which it stood... the vase suddenly fell

44

and was smashed to pieces. I froze in fright and stood motionless before the fragments. My father came in, saw me and said: 'Now look what you've done: we won't have our beautiful vase any more; there's nothing that can put it right now.' I began to sob. It seemed to me that I had committed a crime.

I grew up – and thoughtlessly broke a vessel a thousand times more precious...

I tell myself in vain that I could not have expected so instantaneous a denouement, that I was shocked myself by its suddenness, that I did not suspect what sort of creature Vera was. She really did know how to remain silent until the last moment. I should have fled as soon as I felt that I loved her, loved a married woman, but I stayed – and smashed to pieces a beautiful creation, and in dumb despair do I gaze upon my handiwork.

Yes, Yeltsova guarded her daughter jealously. She protected her until the end and, at the first incautious step, carried her off with her to the grave.

It's time to stop... I have not told you even a hundredth part of what I ought, but even that has been enough for me. So let all that has risen to the surface sink again to the bottom of my soul... In ending, I will say to you: I have borne one conviction out of the experience of recent years: life is not a joke and not an amusement, life is not even a pleasure... life is hard labour. Renunciation, constant renunciation – that is its secret meaning, its solution: not the fulfilment of cherished ideas and dreams, no matter how exalted they might be – the fulfilment of his duty, that is what ought to concern a man; unless he has put chains upon himself, the iron chains of duty, he cannot reach the end of his life's journey without falling; whereas in our youth we think: the freer, the better; the further you'll go. Youth can be permitted to think that way, but it is shameful to cheer yourself with a deceit when the stern face of truth has finally looked you in the eye.

Goodbye! Previously I would have added: be happy; now I shall say to you: try to live, it is not as easy as it seems. Remember me, not in times of sadness, but in times of reflection, and preserve in your soul the image of Vera in all its untainted purity... Once again, goodbye!

Your P.B.

NOTES

1. 'Deny yourself, yourself deny'.

2. Manon Lescaut is the eponymous heroine of Abbé Prévost's 1733 novel.

3. *Le Solitaire* by C-V.P. d'Arlincourt (2nd edition, 1821) was in Turgenev's library on his estate at Spasskoye.

4. The works referred to are *Candide*, Voltaire's short novel of 1759; *The Triumphant Chameleon* – a Russian translation from the German of *The Triumphant Chameleon, or A Portrait of the Anecdotes and Characteristics of Count Mirabeau* appeared in Moscow in 1792; and *Le Paysan perverti* – *The Perverted Peasant* (1776) by R. de la Bretonne.

5. 'This book belongs to Mademoiselle Yevdokia Lavrina.'

6. Stich and Karl Seidelmann were both held in high regard by Russian theatre-goers in Berlin in the 1830s and 1840s, while A.G. Radziwill set many of Goethe's pieces to music; his score for *Faust* was first performed in Berlin in 1835, two years after the composer's death.

7. Albano is a small town near Rome.

8. An inhabitant of the district of Trastevere in Rome.

9. French novelist George Sand (1804–76) had the reputation in conservative circles in Russia of an advocate of immoral behaviour in women, but Turgenev was a warm admirer of her work.

10. A slight misquotation from Alexander Pushkin's poem 'A Conversation between Bookseller and Poet' (1824).

11. From 'The Prologue in Heaven', *Faust*, Part I.

12. Pushkin's novel in verse *Yevgeny Onegin* (1823–31), depicting the failure of hero and heroine to find love together, was a major influence on much of Turgenev's work.

13. The third stanza of Fyodor Tyutchev's poem 'The day is closing, night draws near' (1851).

14. 'Rejoice in Life'.

15 'Yellow Pipe Baccy'.

16 From the poem entitled '*Auf dem See*' ('On the Lake').

17. Sir John Franklin (1786–1847) perished in his attempt to discover the Northwest Passage between the Atlantic and Pacific Oceans. Many expeditions were organised in subsequent years to search for traces of his ships and their crews.

18. The reference to P.A. Gaillard de Bataille's *History of Mademoiselle Cronel, Known as Fretillon, Written by Herself* (1739) alongside Manon Lescaut suggests an image of women of dubious moral character.

19. Turgenev is here alluding to Pushkin's narrative poem set in the reign of Peter the Great, *Poltava* (1828).

20. *Was will er an dem heiligen Ort, / Der da… der dort…*
Faust, Part I, Final scene. (Turgenev's note.)

Yakov Pasynkov

It happened in St Petersburg, in winter, on the first day of Shrovetide. I was invited home for lunch by one of my fellow-pupils from boarding-school who had had a reputation when young for being a shrinking violet, but who turned out subsequently to be a man by no means shy. He is already dead now, like the majority of my fellows. Besides me, a certain Konstantin Alexandrovich Asanov had promised to come to lunch, and also a literary celebrity of the time. The literary celebrity kept us waiting, then finally sent a note to say that he would not be coming, and there appeared in his place a little fair-haired gentleman, one of those eternal uninvited guests in which St Petersburg so abounds.

The lunch carried on for a long time; our host did not begrudge the wines, and little by little our heads became heated. Everything that each of us hid in his soul – and who does not hide something in his soul? – came to the surface. The host's face suddenly lost its bashful and reserved expression; his eyes began to shine insolently, and his lips twisted in a vulgar grin; the fair-haired gentleman laughed in what was somehow a nasty way, with a silly squealing; but Asanov surprised me most of all. This man had always been noted for his sense of decorum, but now he suddenly began rubbing his forehead, putting on airs, boasting of his connections, constantly referring to some uncle of his, a very important person... I positively failed to recognise him; he was blatantly mocking us... and all but turning his nose up at our company. Asanov's insolence made me angry.

'Listen,' I said to him, 'if we're such nonentities in your eyes, go and see your eminent uncle. But perhaps he won't let you in?'

Asanov made no reply to me, and continued rubbing his forehead.

'And what sort of people are they?' he said again. 'I mean, they don't mix in any respectable society, they're not acquainted with a single respectable woman, whereas I,' – he exclaimed, dexterously pulling his wallet out from a side-pocket and slapping it with his hand – 'have here a whole bundle of letters from a girl whose like you won't find anywhere in the world!'

Our host and the fair-haired gentleman paid no attention to

Asanov's last words – they were both holding onto each other's buttons and recounting something – but I pricked up my ears.

'Now that's one boast too many, mister eminent-man's-nephew!' I said, moving up close to Asanov. 'You don't have any letters.'

'You think not?' he retorted, giving me a haughty look. 'Well what's this?' He opened up his wallet and showed me ten or so letters addressed in his name… 'Familiar handwriting!' I thought.

I feel a flush of shame rising on my cheeks… this is most distressing for my self-esteem… Who admits willingly to an ignoble act?… But there is nothing for it, I knew in advance when I began my story that I would have to blush to the roots. And so, reluctantly, I must admit that…

The thing is this: I exploited the inebriation of Asanov, who had carelessly tossed the letters onto the tablecloth, awash with champagne (there was a good deal of noise in my own head too), and quickly ran through one of those letters…

My heart contracted inside me… Alas! I was myself in love with the girl who had been writing to Asanov, and now I could no longer be in any doubt that she loved him. All the letters, written in French, breathed tenderness and devotion…

'*Mon cher ami Constantin!*'[1] was how it began… and it ended with the words: 'Be cautious as previously, and I shall be yours or no one's.'

Stunned, as if by a thunderbolt, I sat motionless for some moments, but finally came to my senses, leapt up, and rushed out of the room…

A quarter of an hour later I was already in my apartment.

The Zlotnitsky family was one of the first with whom I became acquainted after my move to St Petersburg from Moscow. It consisted of the father, the mother, two daughters and a son. The father, already grey-haired, but still a fresh, and formerly a military, man, occupied quite an important position, was to be found at work in the morning, slept after lunch, and in the evening played cards at his club… He was rarely at home, spoke little and unwillingly, looked out from under his brows either sullenly or indifferently, and, apart from travel-writing and geography, read nothing, but when taken ill would colour in pictures, locked up in his study, or tease the old grey parrot, Polly. His wife, a sick, consumptive woman with black, sunken eyes and a sharp nose, did not get off the sofa for days on end and was forever embroidering cushions; so far as I could tell, she was rather afraid of her husband, as if she had somehow wronged him at some time. The elder daughter, Varvara, a plump, rosy girl of about eighteen with light-brown hair, was forever sitting by the window, scrutinising passers-by. The young son was being educated at a government establishment, appeared at home only on Sundays and did not like wasting a word either; even the younger daughter, Sofia, the very girl with whom I had fallen in love, was of a taciturn nature. Silence reigned constantly in the Zlotnitskys' house; it was broken only by Polly's piercing cries; but guests soon got used to them and then once more experienced the weight and oppression of the eternal silence. But guests rarely dropped in on the Zlotnitskys: theirs was a dull house. The very furniture, the red wallpaper with a yellowish pattern, the many wicker chairs in the dining-room, the faded worsted cushions scattered on the sofas with their images of girls and dogs, the horned lamps and the gloomy portraits on the walls – all inspired involuntary depression, there was an air of something cold and sour about everything. When I arrived in St Petersburg I considered it my duty to present myself to the Zlotnitskys: they were related to my mother. With difficulty I sat through an hour, and did not return for a long time; but little by little I began to go more and more often. I was attracted by Sofia, whom at first I did not like but with whom, in the end, I fell in love.

She was a girl of no great height, slim, almost thin, with a pale face, thick black hair and large, brown eyes that were always half-closed. Her features, severe and abrupt, especially her compressed lips, expressed firmness and strength of will. She was known in the household as a girl with character... 'She takes after the eldest sister, after Katerina,' said Mrs Zlotnitskaya one day, when sitting alone with me (in her husband's presence she did not dare to mention this Katerina). 'You don't know her: she's in the Caucasus, married. At the age of thirteen, imagine it, she fell in love with her present husband and announced to us there and then that she wouldn't marry another. No matter what we did – nothing was of any use! She waited till she was twenty-three, incensed her father, and in the end married her idol. We've not got long to wait for something of the sort with Sonechka! May God preserve her from such obstinacy! But I'm afraid for her: she's only just turned sixteen, you know, but already you can't change her...'

Mr Zlotnitsky came in; his wife fell silent straight away.

It was not with her strength of will that Sofia caught my fancy personally – no, for all her dryness, for all her lack of vivacity and imagination, she did have a sort of charm, the charm of directness, honest sincerity and spiritual purity. I respected her just as much as I loved her... It seemed to me that she was also well disposed towards me; to become disenchanted in her attachment, to become convinced of her love for another was painful for me.

The unexpected discovery I had made surprised me all the more as Mr Asanov visited the Zlotnitskys' house infrequently, much more rarely than I, and showed Sonechka no particular favour. He was a handsome, brown-haired man with expressive, albeit rather heavy features, with shining, prominent eyes, a large, white forehead and plump little red lips beneath a thin moustache. He conducted himself extremely modestly, but firmly, spoke and made judgements self-confidently, kept silent with dignity. It was evident that he thought a lot of himself. Asanov laughed rarely and even then through his teeth, and he never danced. He was quite clumsily built. He had once served in the *** Regiment and had a reputation for being an efficient officer.

'It's a strange thing!' I reflected, lying on my sofa. 'How is it that I noticed nothing?...' 'Be cautious as previously': those words from Sofia's letter suddenly came to mind. 'Ah!' I thought, 'that's the way it is! See what a sly young miss! And I thought her frank and sincere... Well, just wait a little, I'll show you...'

But at this point, so far as I can recall, I began to cry bitterly and could not get to sleep all night.

The next day, some time after one o'clock, I set off for the Zlotnitskys'. The old man was out, and his wife was not sitting in her usual place: after eating some pancakes she had developed a headache and had gone to her bedroom to lie down. Varvara was standing with her shoulder leant against the window and looking into the street; Sofia was walking back and forth across the room with her arms folded across her breast;

Polly was making a row.

'Ah, hello!' said Varvara indolently, as soon as I entered the room, and immediately added in a low voice: 'And there goes a man with a tray on his head…' (She was in the habit of occasionally making comments, as though to herself, about passers-by.)

'Hello,' I replied, 'hello, Sofia Nikolayevna. And where's Tatyana Vasilyevna?'

'She's gone for a rest,' said Sofia, continuing to walk around the room.

'We had pancakes,' remarked Varvara, without turning round. 'Why didn't you come?… Where's that clerk going?'

'I didn't have the time.' ('Pre-sent arms!' cried the parrot sharply.) 'What a noise that Polly of yours is making today!'

'He's always making a noise like that,' said Sofia.

We were all silent for a moment.

'Gone through the gate,' said Varvara, then suddenly got up onto the window-sill, and opened the pane at the top.

'What's the matter?' asked Sofia.

'A beggar,' replied Varvara, who bent down, picked up from the window-sill a copper five-kopek coin, on which a grey pile of ash from a smoking candle was still heaped, threw the coin into the street, slammed the window shut, and jumped down heavily onto the floor…

'I had a very nice time yesterday,' I began, sitting down in an armchair, 'I had lunch with a friend; Konstantin Alexandrych was there…' (I looked at Sofia, her brow did not even wrinkle.) 'And I must confess,' I continued, 'we had a real binge: drank about eight bottles between the four of us.'

'Really?' pronounced Sofia calmly, and shook her head.

'Yes,' I continued, rather irritated by her indifference, 'and do you know, Sofia Nikolayevna, it really is true, not for nothing does the saying go: "the truth is in wine".'

'Why's that?'

'Konstantin Alexandrych made us laugh. Just imagine: he suddenly started rubbing his forehead like this and repeating: *What a good boy am I! I've got an eminent uncle!…*'

'Ha-ha!' rang out Varvara's brief, abrupt laugh… 'Polly! Polly! Polly!'

drummed out the parrot in response to her.

Sofia stopped in front of me and looked me in the face.

'And what did you say,' she asked, 'do you remember?'

I blushed involuntarily.

'I don't! I expect I was a fine one too. It really is,' I added, with a significant pause, 'dangerous drinking wine: you go and let out a secret and say something that nobody should know. You regret it later on, but it's already too late.'

'And did you let out a secret?' asked Sofia.

'I'm not talking about myself.'

Sofia turned away and again began walking around the room. I watched her and raged inwardly. 'Just look at that,' I thought, 'a child, a baby, but how she controls herself! Simply made of stone. But just wait...'

'Sofia Nikolayevna,' I said, loudly.

Sofia stopped.

'What do you want?'

'Won't you play something on the piano? By the way, I need to tell you something,' I added in a lower voice.

Without saying a word, Sofia went into the reception hall; I followed her. She stopped by the piano.

'What shall I play for you?' she asked.

'Whatever you like... a Chopin nocturne.'

Sofia began a nocturne. She played quite badly, but with feeling. Her sister played nothing but polkas and waltzes, and those but rarely. She would go up to the piano in her indolent way, sit down, let her burnous slip from her shoulders to her elbows (I never saw her without a burnous), begin playing one polka loudly, not finish, start on another, then suddenly sigh, get up and set off back to the window. A strange creature was that Varvara!

I sat down beside Sofia.

'Sofia Nikolayevna,' I began, looking at her intently from the side, 'I must inform you of a certain piece of news that is unpleasant for me.'

'News? What news?'

'This is what... Until now I have been mistaken in you, completely mistaken.'

'In what way is that?' she said, continuing to play, and with her eyes fixed on her fingers.

'I thought you were frank; I thought you didn't know how to be sly, conceal your feelings, be cunning…'

Sofia's face drew closer to her music.

'I don't understand you.'

'And the main thing,' I continued, 'is that I couldn't possibly have imagined that at your age you already knew how to act out a role so skilfully.'

Sofia's hands began to tremble slightly above the keys.

'What is it you're saying?' she said, still without looking at me. 'I'm acting out a role?'

'Yes, you.' (She smiled… I became furious…) 'You pretend to be indifferent to a certain person and… and then write letters to him,' I added in a whisper.

Sofia's cheeks paled, but she did not turn towards me; she played the nocturne through to the end, rose and closed the lid of the piano.

'Where are you going?' I asked her, not without some embarrassment. 'Aren't you going to answer me?'

'How am I to answer you? I don't know what you're talking about… And I don't know how to pretend.'

She began putting the music away…

The blood rushed to my head.

'No, you know what I'm talking about,' I said, standing up too, 'and if you like, I'll remind you now of some of your expressions in a certain letter: *be cautious as previously…*'

Sofia gave a little start.

'I never expected this from you,' she said finally.

'And I never expected,' I rejoined, 'that you, you, Sofia Nikolayevna, would have favoured with your attention a man who…'

Sofia turned quickly towards me; I involuntarily retreated from her: her eyes, always half-closed, had widened to such an extent that they seemed huge, and they flashed furiously from beneath her brows.

'Ah! If that's the way it is,' she said, 'then know that I love that man and that it's all one to me what opinion you hold of him and of my love for him. And what gave you the idea?… What right do you have to say that?' And if I've made up my mind to do something…'

She fell silent and hurriedly left the reception hall.

I remained. I suddenly felt so awkward and so ashamed that I covered my face with my hands. I understood all the impropriety, all the meanness of my behaviour, and, choking with shame and remorse, I stood as if in disgrace. 'My God,' I thought, 'what have I done!'

'Anton Nikitich,' came the voice of a maid from the hallway, 'would you bring a glass of water quickly for Sofia Nikolayevna.'

'What is it?' answered the pantryman.

'She seems to be crying…'

I shuddered and went into the drawing-room for my hat.

'What were you and Sonechka talking about?' Varvara asked me indifferently; then, after a short silence, added in a low voice: 'There goes that clerk again.'

I started taking my leave.

'But where are you going? Wait: Mummy will be out in a minute.'

'No, I can't, really,' I said, 'better another time.'

At that moment, to my horror, and I mean horror, Sofia stepped firmly into the drawing-room. Her face was paler than normal, and her eyelids were just a little red. She did not even glance at me.

'Look, Sonya,' said Varvara, 'some clerk keeps walking about outside our house.'

'Some sort of spy…' remarked Sofia coldly and scornfully.

This was simply too much! I left and really cannot remember how I dragged myself home.

I was quite wretched, so wretched and bitter that it cannot even be described. In the space of twenty-four hours, two such cruel blows! I had learnt that Sofia loved another and I had lost her respect for ever. I felt crushed and shamed to such an extent that I could not even be indignant with myself. Lying on the sofa and with my face turned towards the wall, I was giving myself up with a certain burning enjoyment to bursts of despairing anguish, when suddenly I heard steps in the room. I raised my head and saw one of my closest friends – Yakov Pasynkov.

I was prepared to be angry with anyone who might enter my room that day, but I could never be angry with Pasynkov; on the contrary, despite the grief that was devouring me, I was inwardly pleased at his arrival and nodded to him. He, as usual, walked around the room a couple of times, grunting and stretching his long limbs, stood in front of me for a while in silence and then sat down in silence in the corner.

I had known Pasynkov for a very long time, almost since childhood. He was educated in that same private boarding-school run by Winterkeller, the German, in which I too spent three years. Yakov's father, a poor retired major, a most honest man, but somewhat unsound in mind, brought him to this German as a seven-year-old boy, paid for him for a year in advance, left Moscow, and proceeded to disappear without trace... Occasionally there were dark, strange rumours about him. Only some eight years later was it ascertained that he had drowned in spring high water while crossing the River Irtysh. What had taken him to Siberia – the Lord knows. Yakov had no other relatives; his mother had died long before. And so he was left on Winterkeller's hands. True, Yakov did have one distant relation, an aunt, but one so poor that she was at first afraid to visit her nephew in case she was saddled with him. Her fear proved unfounded: the kind-hearted German kept Yakov with him, allowed him to study along with the other pupils, fed him (at table, however, he was not served with dessert on weekdays) and had his clothes made out of the worn camlet housecoats (tobacco-coloured, for the most part) of his own mother, an extremely aged but still very spirited and efficient Lithuanian. In consequence of all these circumstances and in consequence of Yakov's subordinate position in the boarding-school generally, his fellows were offhand with him, regarded him superciliously and sometimes called him 'the woman's housecoat', sometimes 'the bonnet's nephew' (his aunt constantly wore the strangest bonnet with a bunch of yellow ribbons sticking up in the shape of an artichoke), sometimes 'Yermak's son' (since his father had drowned in the Irtysh)[2]. But in spite of these nicknames, in spite of his funny clothes and his extreme poverty, everyone was very fond of him, indeed it was impossible not to be fond of him: there was not a kinder, nobler soul, I think, in all the world. He also did very well in his school work.

When I saw him for the first time, he was about sixteen, while I had only just turned thirteen. I was a very vain and spoilt boy, I had grown up in quite a rich household, and for that reason, when I joined the boarding-school, I made haste to become good friends with one little prince, the object of Winterkeller's special attentions, and with two or three other little aristocrats, while putting on airs with all the others. I did not even favour Pasynkov with my attention. This lanky and awkward fellow wearing an ugly jacket and trousers that were too short, from beneath which there peeped thick cotton stockings, seemed to me something like a pageboy from among the house-servants, or the son of a tradesman. Pasynkov was very polite and meek with everyone, although he never tried to ingratiate himself with anybody; if he was rejected, he did not demean himself and did not sulk, but held himself aloof, as though regretfully biding his time. This was how he acted with me as well. Some two months went by. Once, on a clear summer's day, walking from the yard to the garden after a noisy game of ball, I caught sight of Pasynkov sitting on a bench under a tall lilac bush. He was reading a book. I glanced in passing at the binding, and read on the spine the name of Schiller: *Schillers Werke*. I stopped.

'Do you really know German?' I asked Pasynkov…

To this day I begin to feel ashamed when I remember how much disdain there was in the very sound of my voice… Pasynkov quietly raised his small but expressive eyes to look at me and replied, 'Yes, I do; what about you?'

'I'll say!' I retorted, offended now, and I would have gone on my way, but something held me back.

'And what is it exactly you're reading by Schiller?' I asked, with my previous haughtiness.

'Now? I'm reading 'Resignation'[3]: it's a fine poem. Would you like me to read it to you? Sit down here beside me on the bench.'

I wavered a little, but sat down. Pasynkov began reading. He knew German much better than I did: he had to explain the meaning of some of the lines to me, but I was no longer ashamed either of my ignorance, or of his superiority over me. From that day, from that very reading, alone together in the garden in the shade of the lilac, I came to love Pasynkov with all my soul, became good friends with him and subordinated myself to him completely.

I remember his appearance at that time vividly. But then even afterwards he did not change a lot. He was tall, thin, lanky and rather clumsy. Narrow shoulders and a sunken chest gave him a sickly look, although he could not complain about his health. His large head, rounded towards the top, leant slightly to one side, his soft, light-brown hair hung in straggly locks around his slender neck. His face was not handsome and could even appear funny due to his long, plump and reddish nose, which seemed to overhang his wide and straight lips; but his open forehead was fine, and when he smiled, his small grey eyes shone with such meek and affectionate good nature that anyone looking at him would feel warm and cheerful at heart. I also remember his voice, soft and even, with a particularly pleasant sort of huskiness. Generally he spoke little and with noticeable difficulty; but when he became animated, his speech flowed freely and – strange to say! – his voice became still softer; it was as if his gaze retreated inwards and faded away, while the whole of his face was gently aglow. On his lips the words 'goodness', 'truth', 'life', 'learning', 'love', no matter with what rapture they were pronounced, never sounded a false note. Without strain, without effort he entered the realm of the ideal; his chaste soul was ready at any time to stand before 'the sacred beauty's shrine'[4]; it merely awaited the greeting, the touch of another soul... Pasynkov was a romantic, one of the last romantics I happened to meet. Romantics nowadays, as is well known, have almost become extinct; at least, there are none amongst young people today. So much the worse for young people today!

I spent about three years completely at one, as they say, with Pasynkov. I was the confidant of his first love. With what grateful attention and sympathy did I hear out his confessions! The object of his passion was Winterkeller's niece, a sweet, fair-haired little German girl with a plump, almost childish little face and trustingly gentle pale-blue eyes. She was very kind and sentimental, liked Matthison, Uhland[5] and Schiller and declaimed their poetry extremely pleasantly in her shy and resonant voice. Pasynkov's love was the most platonic; he saw his beloved only on Sundays (she came to play forfeits with Winterkeller's children) and had little conversation with her; but once, when she said to him 'mein lieber, lieber Herr Jacob'[6], he could not get to sleep all night because of his excess of well-being. It did not even occur to him then that she said '*mein lieber*' to all his fellows. I also remember his grief and melancholy when the news suddenly spread that Fräulein Friederiche (that was her name) was going to marry Herr Knifftus, the owner of a prospering butcher's shop, a very handsome and even educated man, and was marrying not out of obedience to parental will alone, but also for love. Pasynkov was very wretched then, and he suffered particularly on the day of the young couple's first visit. The former Fräulein, but now already Frau Friederiche presented him once more by the name of '*lieber Herr Jacob*' to her husband, everything about whom was shining: his eyes, his black hair curled up into a quiff, his forehead, his teeth, the buttons on his tailcoat, the chain on his waistcoat, and the very boots on his, incidentally, rather large, splay-toed feet. Pasynkov shook Mr Knifftus by the hand and wished him (and wished him sincerely too – of that I am certain) complete and long-lasting happiness. This took place in my presence. I remember with what surprise and sympathy I gazed then at Yakov. He seemed a hero to me!... And afterwards what sad conversations there were between us! 'Seek solace in art,' I said to him. 'Yes,' he answered me, 'and in poetry.' – 'And in friendship,' I added. 'And in friendship,' he repeated. Oh, happy days!...

It was sad for me to part with Pasynkov! Just before I left, he finally, after a long period of effort and trouble, and after correspondence that was often amusing, received his papers and entered the university. He continued living at Winterkeller's expense, but instead of camlet jackets and trousers he now received normal clothing in reward for the lessons on various subjects that he gave to the younger pupils. Pasynkov never changed the way he treated me right up until the end of my stay at the boarding-school, although the difference in age between us was already beginning to tell and, as I recall, I was starting to be jealous of him in relation to some of his new fellow-students. His influence on me was most salutary. Unfortunately, it did not last long. I shall give just one example. As a child I acquired the habit of lying... I could not bring myself to tell a lie in front of Yakov. But it was a particular joy for me to go for a walk alone with him or to pace up and down the room beside him as, without a glance at me, he recited poetry in his soft and focused voice. It truly seemed to me then that he and I were slowly, little by little, becoming detached from the earth and carried away somewhere, to some radiant, mysterious wonderland... I remember one evening. He and I were sitting under that same lilac bush: we had come to love that spot. All our fellows were already asleep, but we had got up quietly, fumbled our way into our clothes in the darkness and stolen out 'to dream a little'. It was quite warm outside, but a fresh breeze blew at times and made us huddle up still closer to one another. We talked, we talked a great deal and with fervour, so that we even interrupted each other, although we did not argue. Countless stars shone in the sky. Yakov raised his eyes and, gripping my hand, exclaimed softly:

> '*Above us*
> *Heaven and the stars eternal...*
> *And then above the stars their Maker...*'

A reverential tremor ran through me; I turned quite cold and fell onto his shoulder... My heart was overflowing...

Where are those raptures? Alas! Where youth is too.

I met Yakov in St Petersburg some eight years later. I had just joined the civil service and somebody had got him a position in some government department. Our meeting was the most joyous. I shall never forget the moment when, sitting at home one day, I suddenly heard his voice in the entrance hall... How I jumped, with what a beating heart did I leap up and throw myself upon his neck, without giving him the time to take off his fur coat and unwind his scarf! How greedily I gazed at him through involuntary, bright tears of emotion! He had aged a little in the last seven years; wrinkles, fine as the trace of a needle, furrowed his brow here and there, his cheeks had sunk slightly, and his hair was thinner, but there was almost no more growth of beard and his smile remained the same; and his laughter, the dear, inner, seemingly breathless laughter, remained the same...

My God! What, oh what did we not talk over that day!... How many favourite poems we recited to one another! I started to try and persuade him to move in to live with me, but he would not consent, yet on the other hand he did promise to drop in on me daily, and he kept his promise.

And in his soul Pasynkov had not changed. He stood before me the same romantic as I had known him. No matter how the coldness of life, the bitter cold of experience gripped him, the tender flower that had bloomed early in the heart of my friend survived in all its untouched beauty. There was no sign in him even of sadness, even of pensiveness: he was quiet as before, but ever cheerful in spirit.

In St Petersburg he lived as if in a wilderness, not reflecting on the future and hardly associating with anyone. I introduced him to the Zlotnitskys. He called on them quite often. While not proud, he was not shy either, but even with them, as everywhere, he said little; yet still they came to like him. Even the difficult old man, Tatyana Vasilyevna's husband, treated him affectionately, and both the taciturn girls quickly got used to him.

Sometimes he would arrive, bringing with him in the back pocket of his frock-coat some newly published work, and for a long time would be unable to make up his mind to read it, would keep stretching his neck out to one side, like a bird, looking to check whether he could; finally he would find a space in a corner (he liked sitting in corners generally), get the book out and start to read, at first in a whisper, then louder and louder, occasionally breaking in on himself with brief judgements or exclamations. I noticed that Varvara sat down with him and listened to him more readily than her sister, although, of course, she understood him little: literature did not interest her. She would sometimes sit in front of Pasynkov with her chin resting on her hands, gazing not into his eyes, but generally into his face as a whole, and would not utter a word, but only heave a sudden loud sigh. In the evenings we played forfeits, especially on Sundays and on holidays. Then we were joined by two young ladies, sisters, distant relations of the Zlotnitskys, small, round and dreadful gigglers, and by several cadets and officer-cadets, very kind and quiet boys. Pasynkov always sat beside Tatyana Vasilyevna, and together they thought up what had to be done by the person whose turn it was.

Sofia did not like the displays of affection and kisses with which forfeits are generally paid, while Varvara was annoyed when she had to try to find or guess anything. The young ladies giggled away unconcerned – where did they get the laughter from? – and sometimes I was really annoyed, looking at them, but Pasynkov only smiled and shook his head. Old man Zlotnitsky did not get involved in our games and even looked at us not entirely kindly from behind the doors of his study. Only once, quite unexpectedly, did he come out to us and suggest that the person to be drawn should dance a waltz with him; it goes without saying that we agreed. The forfeit was Tatyana Vasilyevna's: she turned quite red, became embarrassed and ashamed like a girl of fifteen – but her husband immediately ordered Sofia to sit down at the piano, he went up to his wife and made two circuits with her, in the old-fashioned way, in triple time. I remember how his bilious and dark face with unsmiling eyes now appeared, now disappeared, turning slowly without altering its stern expression. He took long steps and bobbed up and down while waltzing, whereas his wife took quick little steps and pressed her face against his chest as though in fear. He led her to her seat, bowed to her, went off to his room and closed the door. Sofia tried to get up. But Varvara asked her to continue the waltz, went up to Pasynkov and, reaching out her hand, with an awkward smile said: 'Will you?' Pasynkov was surprised, yet leapt up – he was always known for his refined good manners – and took Varvara by the waist, but slipped at the very first step and, quickly detaching himself from his lady, rolled straight into the cupboard on which the parrot's cage stood... The cage fell off, the parrot took fright and cried out: 'Pre-sent arms!' General laughter broke out... Zlotnitsky appeared on the threshold of his study, gave a stern glance and slammed the door. From that time on one had only to recall this occurrence in Varvara's presence for her immediately to start laughing and look at Pasynkov with such an expression as if anything cleverer than what he had done then would be impossible to imagine.

Pasynkov was very fond of music. He often asked Sofia to play him something, and would sit to one side and listen, occasionally joining in with his thin voice on sentimental notes. He particularly liked Schubert's 'The Stars'[8]. He claimed that when 'The Stars' was played in his presence, it always seemed to him that along with the sounds some long blue rays poured directly into his breast from on high. To

63

this day, at the sight of a cloudless night sky with gently shifting stars, I still always remember Schubert's melody and Pasynkov… One trip out of town also comes to mind. A whole group of us drove in two hired four-seater carriages to Pargolovo. I seem to recall the carriages being taken from Vladimirskaya Street; they were very old, light-blue in colour, on round springs, with wide boxes and wisps of hay inside; the jaded brown horses carried us along at a lumbering trot, each limping on a different leg. We spent a long time strolling through the pine woods around Pargolovo, drank milk from earthenware jugs, and ate wild strawberries with sugar. The weather was wonderful. Varvara did not like to walk a great deal, she soon became exhausted, but on this occasion she did not lag behind us. She took off her hat, her hair came loose, her heavy features became animated, and her cheeks turned red. On meeting two peasant girls in the wood, she suddenly seated herself on the ground, called them over and, although she did not say anything nice to them, sat them down beside her. Sofia looked at them from a distance with a cold smile and did not approach them. She was walking with Asanov, but Zlotnitsky remarked that Varvara was a real mother hen. Varvara stood up and walked away. She went up to Pasynkov several times during the trip and said to him: 'Yakov Ivanych, I want to tell you something,' – but what she wanted to tell him remained unknown.

However, it is time I returned to my story.

I was pleased that Pasynkov had come; but when I remembered what I had done the day before, I became inexpressibly ashamed, and I hurriedly turned back to the wall once more. After a little while Yakov asked me if I was well.

'Yes,' I replied, through gritted teeth, 'only I've got a headache.'

Yakov made no reply and picked up a book. More than an hour passed; I already meant to confess everything to Yakov… Suddenly the bell rang in the entrance hall.

The door onto the staircase was opened… I listened intently… Asanov was asking my man whether I was at home.

Pasynkov stood up; he did not like Asanov and, whispering to me that he would go and have a lie-down on my bed, he set off into my bedroom.

A minute later Asanov came in.

From his flushed face alone, from his perfunctory and dry bow I guessed that he had come to see me not without good reason. 'What's it going to be?' I thought.

'My dear sir,' he began, sitting down quickly in an armchair, 'I've come to see you so that you might resolve a certain doubt for me.'

'Namely?'

'Namely: I wish to know whether you are a man of honour.'

I flared up.

'What does that mean?' I asked.

'This is what it means…' he said, as though hammering out every word, 'yesterday I showed you a wallet of letters to me from a certain person… Today you repeated to that person with reproach – with reproach, note – a number of expressions from those letters, having not the least right to do so. I wish to know how you explain this?'

'And I wish to know what right *you* have to question me?' I replied, trembling all over from fury and inner shame. 'It was your own choice to show off about your uncle, your correspondence; what have I got to do with it? All your letters are intact, aren't they?'

'The letters are intact; but I was in such a condition yesterday that you could easily have…'

'In short, my dear sir,' I began, intentionally speaking as loudly as possible, 'please leave me in peace, do you hear? I don't want to know anything, and I don't intend explaining anything to you. Go and ask that person for explanations!' (I felt my head beginning to spin.)

Asanov directed at me a gaze to which he evidently sought to lend an expression of mocking shrewdness, plucked at his moustache and rose unhurriedly.

'Now I know what to think,' he said, 'your face gives you away more than anything. But I should point out to you that honourable people don't behave like this… To read a letter by stealth and then go bothering an honourable girl…'

'Go to the devil!' I shouted, stamping my feet, 'and send me your second; I don't intend speaking to you.'

'Please don't lecture me,' said Asanov, coldly, 'and I myself intended to send you my second.'

He left. I fell onto the sofa and covered my face with my hands.

Somebody touched me on the shoulder; I removed my hands – before me stood Pasynkov.

'What's this? Is it true?' he asked me. 'Did you read another person's letter?'

I did not have the strength to answer him, but gave my head an affirmative nod.

Pasynkov went up to the window and, standing with his back to me, said: 'You read a girl's letter to Asanov. Who was this girl then?'

'Sofia Zlotnitskaya,' I replied, in the way an accused man answers a judge.

For a long time Pasynkov did not utter a word.

'Only passion can to a certain extent excuse you,' he began at last. 'Are you really in love with Zlotnitskaya?'

'Yes.'

Pasynkov was again silent for a moment.

'I thought so. And today you went to see her and began reproaching her…'

'Yes, yes, yes…' I said despairingly. 'Now you can despise me…'

Pasynkov passed up and down the room a couple of times.

'And does she love him?' he asked.

'She does…'

Pasynkov lowered his head and gazed motionless for a long time at the floor.

'Well, this needs to be helped along,' he began, raising his head, 'it can't be left like this.'

And he picked up his hat.

'And where are you going?'

'To see Asanov.'

I leapt up from the sofa.

'But I won't let you. For pity's sake! How can you? What will he think?'

Pasynkov looked at me.

'So is it really better then, in your view, to set this silliness in motion, destroy yourself, have a young girl disgraced?'

'But what will you say to Asanov?'

'I'll try to make him see sense, I'll say that you ask his forgiveness…'

'But I don't want to apologise to him!'

'You don't want to? Are you not at fault then?'

I looked at Pasynkov: I was struck by his calm and stern, albeit sad expression; it was new to me. I made no reply and sat down on the sofa.

Pasynkov went out.

With what terrible anguish did I await his return! With what cruel slowness did the time pass! He finally returned – it was late.

'Well?' I asked in a timid voice.

'Thank God!' he replied. 'Everything's settled.'

'You've been to Asanov's?'

'Yes.'

'What was he like? Difficult, I expect?' I said, with an effort.

'No, I couldn't say that. I expected worse… He… he's not such a vulgar man as I thought he was.'

'Well, and other than him, you've not called on anyone?' I asked, after a slight pause.

'I called on the Zlotnitskys.'

'Ah!…' (My heart began beating hard. I did not dare look Pasynkov in the eye.) 'How is she?'

'Sofia Nikolayevna – is a sensible girl, good… Yes, she's a good girl. At first she felt awkward, but then she relaxed. Still, our entire conversation lasted no more than five minutes.'

'And you… told her everything… about me… everything?'

'I said what was necessary.'

'I won't be able to go and visit them any more now!' I said mournfully…

'Why's that then? No, you can, occasionally. On the contrary, you ought to go and see them without fail, so that nothing should be thought…'

'Oh, Yakov, you're going to despise me now!' I exclaimed, scarcely holding back my tears.

'Me? Despise you?…' (His affectionate eyes lit up with love.) 'Despise you… silly man! Has it been easy for you, then? Aren't you suffering?'

He reached out his hand to me, I threw myself on his neck, and burst into sobs.

After a few days, in the course of which I could see that Pasynkov was very much out of sorts, I resolved at last to call on the Zlotnitskys. What I felt as I stepped into their drawing-room is difficult to convey in words; I remember that I could hardly make out faces and my voice broke in my chest. And it was no easier for Sofia: she was visibly forcing herself to enter into conversation with me, but her eyes avoided mine just as mine did hers, and in every one of her movements, in the whole of her being, could be discerned constraint mixed with... why hide the truth? – with secret loathing. I sought to relieve both her and myself of such distressing sensations as quickly as possible. This meeting was, fortunately, the last... before her marriage. A sudden change in my fate drew me away to the other end of Russia, and it was for a long time that I said goodbye to St Petersburg, the Zlotnitsky family and, what was for me most painful of all, to good Yakov Pasynkov.

2

Some seven years passed. I do not consider it necessary to relate precisely what happened to me during all that time. How I roamed across Russia, though, paying visits to the back of beyond, and thank God too! The back of beyond is not so terrible as some people think, and in the best hidden spots of dense forest, beneath fallen trees and brushwood, fragrant flowers grow.

One day in spring, while travelling on matters of business through a small district town in one of the distant provinces in the east of Russia, through the dull glass of my tarantas I caught sight of a man in front of a shop on the square whose face seemed to me extremely familiar. I looked closely at this man and, to my no small delight, recognised in him Yelisei, Pasynkov's servant.

I immediately ordered the coachman to stop, leapt out of the tarantas, and went up to Yelisei.

'Hello, my friend!' I said, concealing my excitement with difficulty: 'Are you here with your master?'

'With my master,' he said slowly, then suddenly exclaimed: 'Ah, is it you, sir? I didn't even recognise you!'

'Are you here with Yakov Ivanych?'

'With him, sir, with him... Who else would I be with?'

'Take me to him quickly.'

'As you say, as you say! This way, if you please, this way... We've put up here at the inn.'

And Yelisei led me across the square, constantly repeating: 'Well now, how pleased Yakov Ivanych will be!'

This Yelisei, a man of Kalmuck origins, was extremely ugly and even savage to look at, but he was most kind-hearted and not stupid, he loved Pasynkov passionately, and had served him for about ten years.

'How's Yakov Ivanych's health?' I asked him.

Yelisei turned his small, dark-yellow face towards me.

'Ah, it's bad, sir... it's bad, sir! You won't recognise him... It doesn't look as if he's got long left to live in this world. That's the reason why we're stuck here, otherwise we were travelling to Odessa, you know, to get treatment.'

'And where are you travelling from?'

'From Siberia, sir.'

'From Siberia?'

'That's right, sir. Yakov Ivanych was serving there, sir. That's where he got his wound, sir.'

'Has he joined the military, then?'

'Oh no, sir. He was in the civil service, sir.'

'What strange goings-on!' I thought. Meanwhile we had come close to the inn, and Yelisei ran on ahead to announce me. In the first years of our separation Pasynkov and I had corresponded quite frequently, but I had received his last letter some four years earlier and knew nothing of him since then.

'This way please, sir, this way please!' Yelisei called to me from the stairs. 'Yakov Ivanych very much wants to see you, sir.'

I hurriedly ran up the shaky steps, went into a small, dark room – and my heart turned over inside me... On a narrow bed, underneath his greatcoat, as pale as a dead man, lay Pasynkov, reaching out to me a bare, emaciated arm. I rushed to him and hugged him convulsively.

'Yasha!' I exclaimed at last. 'What's the matter with you?'

'Nothing,' he replied in a weak voice, 'just a little under the weather.

What chance brought you here?'

I sat down on the chair beside Pasynkov's bed and, without letting his hands out of mine, I began looking into his face. I recognised the features dear to me: the expression of his eyes and his smile had not changed; but what had illness done to him!

He noticed the impression he had made on me.

'I've not shaved for three days or so,' he said, 'well, and my hair's not combed either, otherwise I'm... still not so bad.'

'Please, Yasha, tell me,' I began, 'what's this that Yelisei told me?... Are you wounded?'

'Oh! That's a story in itself,' he said. 'I'll tell you later. It's quite true, I'm wounded, and just imagine, by what? An arrow.'

'An arrow?'

'Yes, an arrow, only not a mythological one, not Cupid's dart, but a real arrow of some very flexible wood, with an expertly made arrowhead on the end... Such an arrow produces a very unpleasant sensation, especially when it hits the lungs.'

'But how did it happen? For pity's sake...'

'Like this. You know there were always a lot of funny things in my fate. Do you remember my comical correspondence on the matter of procuring my papers? Now I've been wounded in a funny way. And indeed, what decent man in our enlightened century would allow himself to be wounded by an arrow? And not by accident – take note, not during some games or other, but in a conflict.'

'But you're still not telling me...'

'Just wait a moment,' he interrupted me. 'You know that soon after your departure from St Petersburg I was transferred to Novgorod. I spent quite a long while in Novgorod and, I must confess, I was bored, although I did meet a certain creature there...' he sighed. 'Still it's not the time for that now; but about two years ago a splendid post turned up for me, a little far away, it's true, in the Irkutsk area, but that's not so bad! Evidently my father and I were fated to see Siberia. It's a fine country, Siberia! Rich, free and easy – anyone will tell you that. I liked it there very much. I had non-Russian people under me; a quiet lot, but to my cost they took it into their heads, about ten of them, no more, to transport some contraband. I was sent to intercept them. I intercepted them right enough, only one of them, being stupid, I suppose, decided to defend himself and went and treated me to this arrow... I almost died, but I recovered. Now here I am going to get completely cured... My superiors – may God grant them all good health – supplied the money.'

Pasynkov lowered his head onto the pillow in exhaustion and fell silent. A slight flush spread across his cheeks. He closed his eyes.

'He can't talk much,' said Yelisei, who had not left the room, in a low voice.

Silence fell; all that could be heard was the sick man's heavy breathing.

'And so,' he continued, when he had opened his eyes once again, 'here I am sitting in this rotten little town for a second week... I must have caught a cold. I'm being treated by the local district doctor – you'll see him; he seems to know his business. Anyway, I'm very pleased about this happening, otherwise how would I have met up with you?' (And he took me by the hand. His hand, only recently as cold as ice, was now on fire.) 'You tell me something about yourself,' he began once more, throwing his greatcoat off his chest, 'after all, we last saw one another God knows when.'

I made haste to carry out his wish, anything to stop him talking, and started my account. At first he listened to me with great attention, then asked for a drink, before again beginning to close his eyes and toss his head about on the pillow. I advised him to go to sleep for a while, adding that I would not be travelling on until he had recovered, and would put up in a room alongside his.

'It's very unpleasant here...' Pasynkov tried to begin, but I put my hand over his mouth, then quietly went out.

Yelisei followed me out as well.

'What is this, Yelisei? He's dying, isn't he?' I asked his faithful servant.

Yelisei only waved his hand and turned away.

After dismissing the coachman and hurriedly moving into the adjacent room, I went to see whether Pasynkov had fallen asleep. By his door I bumped into a tall man, very fat and bulky. His face, pock-marked and flabby, expressed indolence – and nothing more; his tiny little eyes were simply stuck together, and his lips shone as if after sleep.

'Allow me to enquire,' I asked him, 'whether you are not the doctor?'

The fat man looked at me, earnestly raising his beetling forehead a little with his eyebrows.

'Indeed I am, sir,' he said at last.

'Do me a service, doctor, would you mind coming in here, into my room? Yakov Ivanych seems to be asleep now; I'm his friend and should like to have a talk with you about his illness which worries me a great deal.'

'Very well, sir,' replied the doctor, with such an expression as if he wished to say: 'What makes you talk so much; I'd have come anyway,' – and he set off after me.

'Tell me please,' I began, as soon as he had lowered himself onto a chair, 'is my friend's condition dangerous? What do you find?'

'Yes,' the fat man calmly replied.

'And… is it very dangerous?'

'Yes, it's dangerous.'

'So that he might… even die?'

'He might.'

I confess, I gave my interlocutor a look almost of hatred.

'Then for pity's sake,' I began, 'some measures must be resorted to, a consultation summoned or something… After all, you can't just… For pity's sake!'

'A consultation, that's possible. Why not? That's possible. Call in Ivan Yefremych…'

The doctor spoke with an effort and sighed constantly. His stomach rose noticeably when he spoke, as if pushing out every word.

'Who is Ivan Yefremych?'

'The town doctor.'

'Shouldn't we send to the provincial centre – what do you think? There must be good doctors there.'

'Yes? That's possible.'

'And who is considered the best doctor there?'

'The best? Kohlrabus was the doctor there… only he was due to be transferred somewhere. But then to tell the truth, it really isn't necessary to send for anyone.'

'Why's that?'

'Even the doctor from the provincial centre won't be any help to your friend.'

'Is he really so ill?'

'Indeed he is, he's done for.'

'So what exactly is wrong with him?'

'He received a wound… His lungs, you know, were damaged… well and then he caught a cold as well, developed a fever… well and so on. And there's no reserves: without reserves, you know it yourself, a man can't manage.'

We were both silent for a moment.

'We could try homeopathy, perhaps…' said the fat man, throwing me a sidelong glance.

'What do you mean, homeopathy? You're an allopath, aren't you?'

'Well what if I am an allopath? Do you think I don't know homeopathy? As well as the next man. Our pharmacist here gives homeopathic treatment, but he doesn't even have any degree.'

'Well,' I thought, 'things are bad!'

'No, doctor,' I said, 'better you treat him according to your normal method.'

'As you wish, sir.'

The fat man stood up and sighed.

'Are you going in to him?' I asked.

'Yes, I need to have a look at him.'

And he went out.

I did not follow him: to see him at the bedside of my poor sick friend was beyond my strength. I called my man and ordered him to go immediately to the provincial centre, to ask there for the best doctor and to be sure to bring him back. There was a knocking in the corridor; I quickly opened the door.

The doctor was already coming out of Pasynkov's room.

'Well?' I asked him in a whisper.

'Nothing really, I've prescribed a mixture.'

'I took the decision, doctor, to send to the provincial centre. I don't doubt your skill, but you know yourself: two heads are better than one.'

'Well then, that's praiseworthy!' said the fat man, and started going downstairs. He was evidently getting tired of me.

I went into Pasynkov's room.

'Did you see the local Aesculapius[9]?' he asked me.

'I did,' I replied.

'What I like about him,' began Pasynkov, 'is his astonishing calmness. A doctor should be a phlegmatic, shouldn't he? It's very encouraging for the patient.'

It goes without saying I did not think of arguing with him.

Towards the evening, contrary to my expectations, Pasynkov felt better. He asked Yelisei to set up the samovar, announced to me that he would be treating me to tea and would drink a cup himself, and became noticeably more cheerful. However, I still tried not to let him talk, and, seeing that he did not want to relax at all, I asked him whether he wanted me to read him anything.

'Like at Winterkeller's, remember?' he replied. 'If you would, with pleasure. What shall we read then? Have a look, will you, the books are over there on my window-sill…'

I went over to the window and picked up the first book that came to hand…

'What is it?' he asked.

'Lermontov.'

'Ah! Lermontov! Splendid! Pushkin's greater, of course… Do you remember: "Now once more have storm clouds gathered in the silence o'er my head…" or: "Now for the final time I dare your sweet image in my thoughts to kiss".[10] Ah, wonderful, wonderful! But Lermontov's good too. You know what, old fellow, go on and open it up at random and read!'

I opened up the book and became embarrassed: I had fallen upon 'The Testament'". I was about to turn over the page, but Pasynkov noticed my movement and said hurriedly: 'No, no, no, read what came up.'

There was nothing for it: I read 'The Testament'.

'It's a fine thing!' said Pasynkov, as soon as I had uttered the last line. 'A fine thing! But it's strange,' he added after a short silence, 'strange that it was "The Testament" in particular that you came upon… Strange!'

I began to read another poem, but Pasynkov was not listening to me, he was gazing off in another direction and repeated another couple of times: 'Strange!'

I lowered the book onto my lap.

'*There is a girl who lives nearby*,'[11] he whispered, and then turning to me, he suddenly asked: 'Well then, do you remember Sofia Zlotnitskaya?'

I blushed.

'How could I fail to remember her!'

'She got married, didn't she?'

'To Asanov, ages ago. I wrote to you about it.'

'That's right, that's right, you wrote. Did her father forgive her in the end?'

'He did, but he wouldn't receive Asanov.'

'Stubborn old man! Well, and what's the word, are they happy together?'

'I really don't know... happy, I think. They live in the country in the *** Province; I haven't seen them, but I've travelled past.'

'And do they have children?'

'I think they have... By the way, Pasynkov?' I questioned.

He glanced towards me.

'Admit it; you didn't want to answer my question then, as I recall: you told her that I loved her, didn't you?'

'I told her everything, the whole truth... I always told her the truth. To be secretive with her – that would be a sin!'

Pasynkov was silent for a moment.

'Well, tell me then,' he began again, 'did you soon stop loving her or not?'

'Not soon, but I did stop loving her. What's the use of sighing in vain?'

Pasynkov turned his face back towards me.

'Whereas I, old fellow,' he began, and his lips started to quiver, 'am no match for you: I still haven't stopped loving her.'

'What!' I exclaimed in inexpressible astonishment: 'So did you love her, then?'

'I did,' pronounced Pasynkov slowly and drew both hands up behind his head. 'How I loved her, that God alone knows. I've told

nobody about it, nobody in the world, and I intended to tell nobody…
but so be it! *I have but little left, they say, to live upon this earth…*[12] It's
not so bad!'

Pasynkov's unexpected confession had so surprised me that I could
say absolutely nothing, but only thought: 'Is it possible? How is it that I
didn't suspect it?'

'Yes,' he continued, as though talking to himself, 'I loved her. I didn't
stop loving her, even when I learnt that her heart belonged to Asanov.
But it was hard for me to learn that! If she'd fallen in love with you, I
would at least have been glad for you; but Asanov… What could she
have liked about him? His good fortune! But betray her feeling, stop
loving, that she simply couldn't do. An honest soul doesn't change…'

I recalled Asanov's visit after the fateful lunch, Pasynkov's inter-
vention, and involuntarily clasped my hands together.

'You learnt it all from me, you poor fellow!' I exclaimed. 'And still
you took it upon yourself to go and see her then!'

'Yes,' Pasynkov began again, 'that conversation with her… I shall
never forget it. That was when I learnt, that was when I understood the
meaning of the word I had long ago picked out: 'Resignation'. Yet still
she remained my constant dream, my ideal… And pitiful is the man
who lives without an ideal!'

I gazed at Pasynkov: his eyes, which seemed to be directed into
the distance, shone with a feverish lustre.

'I loved her,' he continued, 'I loved her – her: calm, honest, inaccessible, incorruptible; when she went away, I almost went mad with
grief… Since then I've loved absolutely no one…'

And suddenly, turning away, he pressed his face against the pillow
and quietly began to cry.

I leapt up, bent down towards him and started to comfort him…

'It's fine,' he said, raising his head a little and giving his hair a shake,
'it's just that I felt a little bitter, a little sorry… for myself, that is… But
it's all fine. It's all the poetry's fault. Come on, read me some more,
something a bit more cheerful.'

I picked up the Lermontov, started turning the pages over quickly;
but, almost as if on purpose, I kept coming upon poems which might
upset Pasynkov. Finally I read him 'The Gifts of the Terek'.

'Rhetorical blather!' my poor friend pronounced in the tones of a mentor: 'Yet there are some good bits. I tried to launch into poetry myself in your absence, old fellow, and started one poem: "The Chalice of Life" – nothing came of it! It's our business to empathise, old fellow, not to create... But I'm tired somehow; I'll have a little sleep – what do you think? What a splendid thing it is to sleep and dream, just think! The whole of our life is a dream and the best thing in it is, again, dreaming.[13]'

'And poetry?' I asked.

'And poetry is a dream too, only a heavenly one.'

Pasynkov closed his eyes.

I stood for a little while at his bedside. I did not think he could fall asleep quickly, yet his breathing was becoming more even and more drawn out. I left on tiptoe, returned to my room and lay down on the sofa. I thought for a long time about what Pasynkov had told me, remembered many things, marvelled, and finally fell asleep myself...

Somebody nudged me; I came to: before me stood Yelisei.

'Please come to the master,' he said.

I got up straight away.

'What's the matter with him?'

'He's raving.'

'Raving? Has he not been like this previously?'

'He has, he was raving last night too, only today it's something awful.'

I went into Pasynkov's room. He was not lying, but sitting on his bed with the whole of his trunk bent forward, spreading his hands, smiling and talking, constantly talking in an inaudible and weak voice like the rustling of reeds. His eyes were wandering. The sad glow of the night-light, set down on the floor and shielded with a book, lay in a motionless patch on the ceiling; Pasynkov's face seemed even paler in the semi-darkness.

I went up to him, called him – he did not respond. I started to listen closely to his babbling: he was raving about Siberia, about its forests. There was sense at times in his ravings.

'What trees!' he whispered. 'Right up to the sky. How much frost there is on them! Silver... Snowdrifts... And here are some little

77

tracks... first a hare was hopping about, then a white ermine... No, it was my father ran by with my papers. There he is... There he is! Got to go; the moon's shining. Got to go and find the papers... Ah! A flower, a scarlet flower – Sofia's there... There, the little bells are ringing, then it's the frost ringing... Oh no, it's silly bullfinches hopping about in the bushes, whistling... See them, with their red breasts! It's cold... Ah! There's Asanov... Ah yes, he's a cannon, isn't he – a bronze cannon, and he has a green gun-carriage. That's why he's liked. Did a star tumble? No, it's an arrow flying... Ah, how quick, and straight to my heart!... Who was it that fired? You, Sonechka?'

He bent his head and started whispering incoherent words. I glanced at Yelisei: he was standing with his hands behind his back, gazing pitifully at his gentleman.

'Well then, old fellow, have you become a practical man?' he suddenly asked, directing such a clear, such a conscious look at me, that I gave an involuntary start and was about to reply, but he continued straight away: 'Whereas I, old fellow, haven't become a practical man, haven't become one, what can you do? I was born a dreamer, a dreamer! A dream, a dream... What is a dream? Sobakevich's peasant[14] – that's a dream. Oh!...'

Pasynkov raved almost right through until morning; at last he quietened down little by little, sank back onto his pillow and began to doze. I returned to my room. Worn out by the cruel night, I fell into a deep sleep.

Yelisei woke me up once again.

'Ah, sir!' he said with a tremor in his voice. 'I think Yakov Ivanych is dying.'

I ran in to Pasynkov. He was lying motionless. By the light of the breaking day he already seemed like a dead man. He recognised me.

'Farewell,' he whispered, 'give her my greetings, I'm dying...'

'Yasha!' I exclaimed, 'enough of that! You're going to live...'

'No, how could I! I'm dying... Here, take this as a memento...' (He pointed at his chest.) 'What's that?' he suddenly began. 'Just look: the sea... all golden, and upon it blue islands, marble temples, palm trees, incense...'

He fell silent... stretched himself out...

Half an hour later he was no more. Yelisei fell sobbing at his feet. I closed his eyes.

Round his neck he had a small silk amulet on a black lace. I took it for myself.

He was buried on the third day... The noblest heart was hidden for ever in the grave! I myself threw the first handful of earth on top of him.

3

Another year and a half passed. Business matters obliged me to travel to Moscow. I put up in one of the good hotels there. One day, while walking along the corridor, I glanced at the blackboard with the names of guests and almost cried out in astonishment: against room number twelve, written clearly in chalk, stood the name of Sofia Nikolayevna Asanova. I had recently chanced to hear a lot of bad things about her husband; I had learnt that he had developed a passion for wine and cards, was ruined financially and was generally behaving badly. His wife was spoken of with respect... Not without excitement did I return to my room. A passion that had long grown cold seemed to stir in my heart which began beating hard. I made up my mind to go and see Sofia Nikolayevna. 'How much time has passed since the day of our parting!' I thought. 'She's probably forgotten everything that happened between us then.'

I sent Yelisei, whom I had taken into my service after Pasynkov's death, to leave her my visiting-card, and told him to ask whether she was at home and whether I could see her. Yelisei soon returned and announced that Sofia Nikolayevna was at home and receiving visitors.

I set off to see Sofia Nikolayevna. When I went in, she was standing in the middle of the room and saying goodbye to some tall, thickset gentleman. 'As you wish,' he was saying in a deep, booming voice, 'he is not a harmless man, he is an unproductive man; and any unproductive man in a well-ordered society is harmful, harmful, harmful!'

With these words the tall gentleman left. Sofia Nikolayevna turned to me.

'How long it is since we last met!' she said. 'Sit down, please...'

We sat down. I looked at her... To see after a long separation the features of a face that was once dear, perhaps beloved, and to recognise, yet not recognise them, as if through the former, still not forgotten appearance there protruded another that, albeit similar, is alien; to notice instantly, almost involuntarily, the traces applied by time – this is all rather sad. 'And I too must have changed,' everyone thinks to himself...

Sofia Nikolayevna, however, had not aged a lot; but when I had seen her for the last time she had just turned sixteen, and since then nine years had passed. Her features had become even more correct and severe; as before, they expressed sincerity of feelings and firmness, but instead of the former calm, they spoke of some suppressed pain and anxiety. Her eyes had deepened and darkened. She had begun to resemble her mother...

Sofia Nikolayevna was the first to strike up a conversation.

'We've both altered,' she began. 'Where have you been all this time?'

'Roaming here and there,' I replied. 'And have you been living in the country all the time?'

'For the most part in the country. Even now I'm only passing through here.'

'What of your parents?'

'My mother passed away, but my father is still in St Petersburg; my brother's in the civil service; Varya lives with him.'

'And your husband?'

'My husband?' she started speaking in a rather hurried voice. 'He's in southern Russia now, at the fairs. He always loved horses, you know, and he set up his own stud... so in order to... he's buying horses now.'

At this moment there came into the room a girl of about eight with a Chinese hairstyle, with a very sharp and lively little face and large dark-grey eyes. Upon seeing me, she immediately stretched her little leg out, dropped a nimble curtsey and went up to Sofia Nikolayevna.

'Here, let me present you, my daughter,' said Sofia Nikolayevna, touching the little girl under her rounded chin with her finger, 'she didn't want to stay at home for anything, begged me to bring her with me.'

The little girl looked me over with her quick eyes and screwed them up just slightly.

'She's a good girl,' continued Sofia Nikolayevna, 'she's not afraid of anything. And her studies are going well; I have to praise her for that.'

'*Comment se nomme monsieur?*'[15] asked the little girl in a low voice, leaning towards her mother.

Sofia Nikolayevna gave my name. The little girl glanced at me again.

'What's your name?' I asked her.

'My name's Lydia,' the little girl replied, looking me boldly in the eyes.

'I expect they spoil you,' I remarked.

'Who spoils me?'

'What do you mean, *who*? I imagine everybody does, beginning with your parents.' (The little girl looked at her mother in silence.) 'I imagine Konstantin Alexandrych…' I continued.

'Yes, yes,' Sofia Nikolayevna joined in, while her daughter did not take her attentive gaze off her. 'My husband, of course… he's very fond of children.'

A strange expression flashed across Lydia's intelligent little face. Her lips pouted slightly; her head dropped.

'Tell me,' added Sofia Nikolayevna hurriedly, 'you're here on business, are you?'

'On business… And you too?'

'Yes… In your husband's absence, you understand, you get involved in business, like it or not.'

'*Maman!*' Lydia tried to begin.

'*Quoi, mon enfant?*'

'*Non – rien… Je te dirai après.*'[16]

Sofia Nikolayevna laughed and shrugged.

We were both silent for a while, and Lydia crossed her arms on her chest with an air of importance.

'Tell me, please,' began Sofya Nikolayevna once more, 'I seem to remember, you used to have a friend… what was his name now? He had such a kind face… He was always reading poetry; such an enthusiast…'

'Do you mean Pasynkov?'

'Yes, yes, Pasynkov… where is he now?'

'He's dead.'

'Dead?' repeated Sofia Nikolayevna. 'What a shame!…'

'Did I see him?' asked the little girl in a hasty whisper.

'No, Lydia, you didn't see him. What a shame!' repeated Sofia Nikolayevna.

'You feel regret for him…' I began, 'so what if you had known him as I knew him?… But may I ask why you started speaking of him in particular?'

'I really don't know…' (Sofia Nikolayevna lowered her eyes.) 'Lydia,' she added, 'go to your nurse.'

'Will you call me when the time comes?' asked the little girl.

'Yes, I'll call you.'

The little girl left the room. Sofia Nikolayevna turned to me: 'Please tell me all you know about Pasynkov.'

I began telling her. I outlined in brief the whole of my friend's life, tried, so far as I could, to portray his soul, described his last meeting with me, his death.

'And that's what sort of a man,' I exclaimed, finishing my story, 'has left us, unnoticed, scarcely appreciated! And that might not be such a bad thing. What does the appreciation of men signify? But I'm hurt, I'm offended by the fact that such a man, with such a loving and devoted heart, died without once experiencing the bliss of requited love, without exciting sympathy in a single female heart worthy of him!… It's alright if the likes of us don't taste that bliss: we're unworthy of it; but Pasynkov!… And what's more, haven't I met in my lifetime a thousand people who couldn't compare with him in any respect, yet who have been loved? Surely one doesn't have to think that certain deficiencies – brashness, for example, or frivolity – are essential in a man for a woman to become attached to him? Or is love afraid of perfection, such perfection as is possible on earth, as something alien and terrible?'

Sofia Nikolayevna heard me out without taking her severe and penetrating eyes off me and keeping her lips tightly pursed; only her brows were occasionally knitted.

'Why do you assume,' she said, after a short silence, 'that not a single woman fell in love with your friend?'

'Because I know it, I know it for certain.'

Sofia Nikolayevna meant to say something, but stopped. She seemed to be struggling with herself.

'You're mistaken,' she began at last. 'I know a woman who fell ardently in love with your late friend; she loves and remembers him to this day… and word of his death will affect her deeply.'

'Who is this woman, may I know?'

'My sister, Varya.'

'Varvara Nikolayevna!' I exclaimed in astonishment.

'Yes.'

'What? Varvara Nikolayevna?' I repeated. 'That…'

'I'll finish your thought out loud,' continued Sofia Nikolayevna: 'that – in your view – cold, indifferent, limp girl loved your friend: that's why she didn't and won't get married. Until today I alone knew about this: Varya would sooner die than reveal her secret. We know how to suffer in silence in our family.'

I looked at Sofia Nikolayevna intently for a long time, involuntarily reflecting on the bitter significance of her last words.

'You have surprised me,' I said at last. 'But do you know, Sofia Nikolayevna, if I were not afraid of arousing unpleasant memories for you, I in my turn could surprise you too…'

'I don't understand you,' she said slowly and with a certain embarrassment.

'You certainly don't understand me,' I said, hurrying to get up, 'and for that reason, instead of a verbal explanation, allow me to send you a certain item…'

'But what is it?' she asked.

'Don't worry, Sofia Nikolayevna, I'm not talking about myself.'

I bowed and returned to my room, got out the amulet that I had taken off Pasynkov, and sent it to Sofia Nikolayevna with the following note:

My late friend wore this amulet constantly on his breast, and he died with it on. Inside it is a note of yours to him, utterly insignificant in content; you can read it. He wore it because he loved you passionately, something he admitted to me only on the eve of his death. Now that he is dead, why should you not learn that his heart too belonged to you?

Yelisei soon returned and brought me back the amulet.

'What?' I asked. 'Didn't she ask you to say anything to me?'

'Nothing, sir.'

I was silent for a moment.

'Did she read my note?'

'She must have done, sir; her maid took it to her.'

'Inaccessible!' I thought, remembering Pasynkov's last words.

'Well, off you go,' I said out loud.

Yelisei gave a somehow strange smile and did not leave.

'A young woman,' he began, 'has come to see you, sir.'

'What young woman?'

Yelisei was silent for a moment.

'Didn't the late master say anything to you, sir?'

'No... What is it?'

'When he was in Novgorod,' he continued, putting his hand on the lintel, 'he became friends with, roughly speaking, a young woman. So now this young woman wants to see you, sir. I met her in the street the other day. I said to her: "You come along; if the master tells me to, I'll let you in."'

'Ask her in, ask her in, of course. But then... what sort of woman is she?'

'Ordinary, sir... a townswoman... Russian.'

'Did the late Yakov Ivanych love her?'

'He quite loved her, sir. Well, and she... When she heard the master had passed away, she was ever so upset. She's alright, a good girl, sir.'

'Ask her in, ask her in.'

Yelisei went out, then came back straight away. Behind him walked a young woman in a multi-coloured cotton print dress, and with a dark shawl on her head covering half her face. When she saw me, she became embarrassed and turned away.

'What's the matter?' Yelisei said to her. 'Go on, don't be afraid.'

I went up to her and took her by the hand.

'What's your name?' I asked her.

'Masha,' she replied in a quiet voice, stealing a glance at me.

To look at, she appeared to be about twenty-two or twenty-three; she had a round, quite ordinary, but pleasant face, delicate cheeks, meek blue eyes and small hands, very pretty and clean. She was neatly dressed.

'You knew Yakov Ivanych?' I continued.

'I did know him, sir,' she said, pulling at the ends of her shawl, and tears stood out on her eyelids…

I asked her to sit down.

She sat down immediately on the edge of a chair, without excessive shyness or false modesty. Yelisei left the room.

'You met in Novgorod?'

'In Novgorod,' she replied, folding her hands beneath her shawl. 'I only learnt of his death two days ago from Yelisei Timofeyich, sir. When he left for Siberia, Yakov Ivanych promised to write, and he wrote twice, but didn't write any more, sir. I would have followed him even to Siberia, sir, but he didn't want me to.'

'Do you have relatives in Novgorod?'

'Yes.'

'Did you live with them?'

'I lived with my mother and with my married sister; but then my mother got angry with me, and my sister began to feel cramped too: they've got a lot of children; so I moved out. I always pinned my hopes on Yakov Ivanych and wanted nothing other than to see him, and he was always kind to me – you can ask Yelisei Timofeyich.'

Masha was silent for a moment.

'I've even got his letters,' she continued. 'Here, sir, look.'

She took several letters from her pocket and passed them to me.

'Read them, sir,' she added.

I opened up one letter and recognised Pasynkov's handwriting.

Dear Masha! – he wrote in a large, clear hand – *Yesterday you leant your little head against my head, and when I asked: why are you doing that? you said to me: I want to listen to what you're thinking. I'll tell you what I was thinking: I was thinking how good it would be to teach Masha to read and write! She'd be able to make out this letter…*

Masha glanced at the letter.

'He wrote me that while he was still in Novgorod, sir,' she said, 'when he was meaning to teach me to read and write. Look at the others, sir. There's one there from Siberia, sir. Read that one, sir.'

I read the letters. They were all very affectionate, even tender. In one of them, specifically in the first letter from Siberia, Pasynkov called Masha his best friend, promised to send her money for the journey to Siberia and ended with the following words:

> *I kiss your pretty little hands; the girls here don't have such hands; and their heads are no match for yours, and neither are their hearts... Read the books I gave you and remember me, and I shan't forget you. Only you, you alone loved me: and so I want to belong to you alone too...*

'I see he was very attached to you,' I said, returning the letters to her.

'He loved me very much,' said Masha, putting the letters away carefully in her pocket, and tears quietly began to flow down her cheeks. 'I always put my hope in him; if the Lord had prolonged his life, he wouldn't have abandoned me. God grant him eternal life!...'

She wiped her eyes with the end of her shawl.

'And where are you living now?' I asked.

'I'm here now, in Moscow; I came with a lady, but now I'm without a position. I went to see Yakov Ivanych's auntie, but she's very poor herself. Yakov Ivanych often used to talk to me about you, sir,' she added, getting up and bowing, 'he always liked you very much and remembered you. And I met Yelisei Timofeyich two days ago and wondered whether you would like to help me, as I'm now left without a position...'

'With great pleasure, Maria... may I ask your patronymic?'

'Petrovna,' replied Masha and looked down.

'I'll do everything I can for you, Maria Petrovna,' I continued, 'I'm only sorry that I'm just passing through and I don't know many good houses.'

Masha sighed.

'Any position would do me, sir... I don't know how to cut dresses, but I can do any kind of sewing, sir... well, and I can look after children too.'

'I should give her some money,' I thought, 'but how am I to do it?'

'Listen, Maria Petrovna,' I began, not without embarrassment, 'you'll forgive me, please, but you know from Pasynkov how friendly I was with him… Won't you allow me to offer you… in the first instance a small sum of money?'

Masha looked at me.

'What, sir?' she asked.

'Do you need some money?' I said.

Masha turned quite red and bent her head.

'What do I need money for?' she whispered. 'Better find me a position, sir.'

'I'll try to find you a position, but I can't give you a certain reply, and you're wrong to feel ashamed, truly… I'm not some stranger to you, after all… Take it from me in memory of our friend…'

I turned away, hastily took several banknotes from my wallet and offered them to her.

Masha stood motionless, her head lowered still further…

'Do take it,' I repeated.

She quietly raised her eyes to look at me, gave a sad gaze into my face, quietly freed her pale hand from under her shawl and reached it out to me.

I placed the banknotes on her cold fingers. In silence she hid her hand under the shawl once more and lowered her eyes.

'In future as well, Maria Petrovna,' I continued, 'if you need anything, please turn directly to me. I'll let you know my address.'

'I'm humbly grateful, sir,' she said, then after a moment's silence added: 'Did he tell you about me, sir?'

'I met him on the eve of his death, Maria Petrovna. But then I don't remember… I think he did.'

Masha passed her hand over her hair, rested her cheek on it a little, had a think, then, saying, 'Goodbye, sir,' she left the room.

I sat down by the table and began thinking bitter thoughts. This Masha, her relations with Pasynkov, his letters, Sofia Nikolayevna's sister's secret love for him… 'The poor man, the poor man!' I whispered with a heavy sigh. I recalled the whole of Pasynkov's life, his childhood, his youth, Fräulein Friederiche… 'There,' I thought, 'what a lot you were given by fate, what a lot it gave you to enjoy!'

The next day I called on Sofia Nikolayevna again. I was made to wait in the entrance hall and, when I went in, Lydia was already sitting beside her mother. I realised that Sofia Nikolayevna did not wish to renew the conversation of the day before.

We began talking – I really cannot remember about what, about city gossip, about business… Lydia frequently had her say and looked at me slyly. An amusing air of importance would suddenly become apparent on her mobile little face… The clever little girl must have guessed that her mother had sat her down beside her on purpose.

I rose and began to take my farewell. Sofia Nikolayevna saw me to the door.

'I gave you no reply yesterday,' she said, stopping on the threshold, 'but what reply could I have given? Our life does not depend on us; but we all of us have one anchor, from which, unless you yourself wish it, you will never break away: a sense of duty.'

I inclined my head wordlessly as a sign of agreement and said goodbye to the young puritan.

All that evening I remained at home, but I did not think about her: I was thinking, constantly thinking about my dear, unforgettable Pasynkov – about that last of the romantics; and emotions, at times sad, at times tender, pierced my breast with sweet pain and resounded in the strings of my still not entirely obsolete heart… May you rest in peace, impractical man, good-natured idealist! And God grant all practical gentlemen, to whom you were always alien and who will perhaps now even laugh at your shadow, God grant they all taste but a hundredth part of those pure pleasures by which, in defiance of fate and men, your poor and humble life was enriched!

NOTES

1. 'My dear friend Konstantin.'

2. Yermak was a Cossack who participated prominently in the Russian expansion into Siberia until his death by drowning in 1585.

3. Friedrich von Schiller's poem 'Resignation' was a key work for many of Turgenev's Russian contemporaries; the title was variously translated into Russian as, for example, 'Renunciation' or 'Obedience to Fate'.

4. The closing line of Pushkin's poem 'The Beauty' (1832).

5. Friedrich Matthison (1761–1831) and Johann Uhland (1787–1862), German poets.

6. 'My dear, dear Mr Yakov'.

7. A slight misquotation from Ivan Kozlov's poem 'To my Friend V.A. Zh[ukovsky]' (1825).

8. Franz Schubert's 1811 setting of a poem by Friedrich Klopstock (1724–1803).

9. In Greek mythology, Aesculapius, the son of Apollo, the god of medicine was a healer and physician who himself became a demigod.

10. The first lines are the opening to Pushkin's poem 'Presentiment' (1828), and the second quotation is the opening to his poem 'Leave-taking' (1830).

11. A line from Mikhail Lermontov's poem 'The Testament' (1841).

12. Another quotation from Lermontov's 'The Testament'.

13. The allusion is to P. Calderon de la Barca's *Life is a Dream* (1635), a play much admired by Turgenev.

14. Sobakevich is a character in Nikolai Gogol's epic *Dead Souls* (1842) whose imagination endows dead peasants with exaggerated qualities.

15. 'What's the gentleman's name?'

16. 'Mummy!' 'What, my child?' 'No, it's nothing… I'll tell you later.'

Ivan Sergeyevich Turgenev was born in Orel in 1818. His was a lonely childhood, marked by a difficult relationship with his cruel, domineering mother. He studied in Moscow, Berlin and St Petersburg, and as a student became an advocate of the Westernisation of Russia.

In 1843 Turgenev joined the Russian civil service, and it was whilst in employment there that his first works were published. He won acclaim for 'Khor and Kalinych' (1847), a sympathetic story of peasant life which was included in the 1852 collection, *A Sportsman's Sketches*. It has been said that this work in particular was instrumental in Alexander II's decision to emancipate the serfs. From 1850 Turgenev spent considerable time travelling, particularly in Western Europe, and often accompanied by the married singer Pauline Viardot, a lifelong friend. His novels from this period – *Rudin* (1856), *A Nest of Gentlefolk* (1859) and *On the Eve* (1860) among them – are concerned with society and politics; similarly, his masterpiece, *Fathers and Sons* (1862) deals with personal and social rebellion, and it is this that marks him out as different from his contemporaries, in particular Tolstoy and Dostoevsky, whose writings were imbued with a sense of the spiritual and the religious.

During this time Turgenev also penned a number of short stories and plays. 'First Love' (1860) and 'Torrents of Spring' (1872) are notable among his short stories, whilst his finest play is undoubtedly *A Month in the Country* (1855) which was later to influence the writing of Anton Chekhov. Turgenev was the first of the great Russian writers to achieve recognition in Western Europe, mostly due to the fact that he spent much of his time there, and was well acquainted with the likes of Gustave Flaubert, Charles Dickens, George Eliot and George Sand. He visited England many times, and in 1879 he was made an honorary Doctor of Civil Law at Oxford for his role in advancing the cause of the Russian serfs.

Turgenev died at Bougival, near Paris, in 1883. His remains were returned to Russia where they were buried in the Volkovo Cemetery in St Petersburg.

Hugh Aplin studied Russian at the University of East Anglia and Voronezh State University, and worked at the Universities of Leeds and St Andrews before taking up his post as Head of Russian at Westminster School, London. His previous translations include Anton Chekhov's *The Story of a Nobody*, Nikolai Gogol's *The Squabble*, Fyodor Dostoevsky's *Poor People* and Leo Tolstoy's *Hadji Murat*, all published by Hesperus Press.

HESPERUS PRESS – 100 PAGES

Hesperus Press, as suggested by the Latin motto, is committed to bringing near what is far – far both in space and time. Works written by the greatest authors, and unjustly neglected or simply little known in the English-speaking world, are made accessible through new translations and a completely fresh editorial approach. Through these short classic works, each around 100 pages in length, the reader will be introduced to the greatest writers from all times and all cultures.

For more information on Hesperus Press, please visit our website: **www.hesperuspress.com**

ET REMOTISSIMA PROPE

SELECTED TITLES FROM HESPERUS PRESS

Gustave Flaubert *Memoirs of a Madman*

Alexander Pope *Scriblerus*

Ugo Foscolo *Last Letters of Jacopo Ortis*

Anton Chekhov *The Story of a Nobody*

Joseph von Eichendorff *Life of a Good-for-nothing*

Mark Twain *The Diary of Adam and Eve*

Giovanni Boccaccio *Life of Dante*

Victor Hugo *The Last Day of a Condemned Man*

Joseph Conrad *Heart of Darkness*

Edgar Allan Poe *Eureka*

Emile Zola *For a Night of Love*

Daniel Defoe *The King of Pirates*

Giacomo Leopardi *Thoughts*

Nikolai Gogol *The Squabble*

Franz Kafka *Metamorphosis*

Herman Melville *The Enchanted Isles*

Leonardo da Vinci *Prophecies*

Charles Baudelaire *On Wine and Hashish*

William Makepeace Thackeray *Rebecca and Rowena*

Wilkie Collins *Who Killed Zebedee?*

Théophile Gautier *The Jinx*

Charles Dickens *The Haunted House*

Luigi Pirandello *Loveless Love*

Fyodor Dostoevsky *Poor People*

E.T.A. Hoffmann *Mademoiselle de Scudéri*

Henry James *In the Cage*

Francis Petrarch *My Secret Book*

André Gide *Theseus*

D.H. Lawrence *The Fox*

Percy Bysshe Shelley *Zastrozzi*

Marquis de Sade *Incest*

Oscar Wilde *The Portrait of Mr W.H.*

Giacomo Casanova *The Duel*

Leo Tolstoy *Hadji Murat*

Friedrich von Schiller *The Ghost-seer*

Nathaniel Hawthorne *Rappaccini's Daughter*

Pietro Aretino *The School of Whoredom*

Honoré de Balzac *Colonel Chabert*

Thomas Hardy *Fellow-Townsmen*

Arthur Conan Doyle *The Tragedy of the Korosko*

Stendhal *Memoirs of an Egotist*

Katherine Mansfield *In a German Pension*

Giovanni Verga *Life in the Country*

Theodor Storm *The Lake of the Bees*

F. Scott Fitzgerald *The Rich Boy*

Dante Alighieri *New Life*

Guy de Maupassant *Butterball*

Charlotte Brontë *The Green Dwarf*

Elizabeth Gaskell *Lois the Witch*

Joris-Karl Huysmans *With the Flow*

George Eliot *Amos Barton*

Gabriele D'Annunzio *The Book of the Virgins*

Heinrich von Kleist *The Marquise of O–*

Alexander Pushkin *Dubrovsky*